I ORBED, Paige [barcode obscures text] CAT FORM. Now her tail flicked with irritation.

She just hoped Tyler hadn't transported them too far from home. She had never orbed major distances on her own. Judging from the glaring sun, they were somewhere much warmer than San Francisco.

Paige was pretty sure she had orbed them only a few feet, just outside the temple walls. *Make that enormous temple walls*, she amended. Her eyes traveled up, up, and up the massive walls of the massive building.

An even larger structure caught her eye. Looming above the rooftop was a very familiar monument.

The Sphinx. And it looked a lot newer than it did in pictures.

More titles in the

Pocket Books series

All Pocket Books are available by post from:
Simon & Schuster Cash Sales. PO Box 29
Douglas, Isle of Man IM99 1BQ
Credit cards accepted.
Please telephone 01624 836000
fax 01624 670923
Internet http://www.bookpost.co.uk
or email: bookshop@enterprise.net for details

SHADOW OF
THE SPHINX

An original novel by Carla Jablonski

Based on the hit TV series created by

Constance M. Burge

**POCKET
BOOKS**

LONDON • SYDNEY • NEW YORK • TORONTO

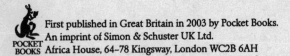
First published in Great Britain in 2003 by Pocket Books.
An imprint of Simon & Schuster UK Ltd.
POCKET
BOOKS Africa House, 64–78 Kingsway, London WC2B 6AH

Originally published in 2003 by Simon Pulse,
an imprint of Simon & Schuster Children's Division, New York

™ Copyright © 2003 by Spelling Television Inc. All Rights Reserved.

POCKET BOOKS and colophon are registered trademarks of Simon & Schuster.
A CIP catalogue record for this book is available from the British Library

ISBN 07434 61045

5 7 9 10 8 6 4

Printed by Cox & Wyman Ltd, Reading, Berkshire

For the Brooklyn Public Library and the Brooklyn Museum, where I spent so much time visiting ancient Egypt

Chapter

1

"**Are you sure** you don't want to come to brunch with us, sweetie?" Phoebe Halliwell stood in the open doorway, bright sunlight streaming into the hallway behind her.

"No, thanks," Paige told her half sister. "You go ahead."

"You're missing a great eggs Benedict," Phoebe tempted.

Paige shook her head, her long dark hair sliding across her shoulder. "Which means I'm also missing about a gazillion calories." She patted her stomach. "It's probably for the best."

Phoebe gave Paige's slim, shapely body a once-over, then rolled her eyes. "As if," she retorted, her brown eyes twinkling. "But okay."

The car horn bleated. Phoebe's fiancé, Cole Porter, stood beside the car, reaching through the driver's side window to honk the horn. He grinned and held up his hands in a *So are we going?* gesture.

Piper's head popped out of the car's back window. "Come on, Phoebe," she called. "You know if we don't get to Sylvio's soon, there'll be a line out the door."

"Go," Paige urged Phoebe. "Have a banana almond muffin for me."

"If you're sure . . ."

Paige took her sister's shoulders firmly and turned her around. "Scoot."

"Okay, okay, I can take a hint."

Paige watched Phoebe dash down the walk— and straight into Cole's arms. He gave her a kiss and then escorted her around to the passenger side of the car. With an exaggerated flourish, he opened her door. Giggling, Phoebe slid into the car. Cole trotted around the front of the car and settled himself behind the wheel.

Without even looking, Paige knew that her other sister, Piper, was snuggled up in the backseat with her husband Leo. This knowledge wasn't a case of witchy telepathy—it was youngest-sister intuition. Based on loads of experience.

Cole gave a good-bye honk as he started up the car. Paige shot them all a bright smile and waved. As they pulled away she stepped back inside the manor and shut the door.

She let out a small sigh. She hadn't been completely truthful with Phoebe. Counting calories wasn't the real reason she chose solitude over Sylvio's Sunday brunch. Okay, it was true that she wasn't exactly a heavy eater first thing in the morning and that eggs coated with thick hollandaise sauce actually made her a bit squeamish before four P.M. But she could have ordered one of Sylvio's killer muffins and fruit smoothies. No. The reason she opted out was that she needed a break from her new and not-so-exalted role as official fifth wheel. A girl could use some alone time now and then.

Not that she wasn't happy for Phoebe and Piper. It was great to see that true love and committed relationships were possible for a witch—even if those partners in passion were a former demon and a Whitelighter. In fact, most of the time the Leo-and-Piper/Phoebe-and-Cole show gave her hope. Since Paige's powers as a witch had been activated, she had discovered that her destiny as a Charmed One dedicated to protecting innocents put a real crimp in her social life. So seeing that Piper had married Leo despite all the obstacles, and that Phoebe had become engaged to a former enemy, well, maybe, just maybe, there would be someone out there for Paige who could deal with the whole Charmed Ones thing.

Though how any normal second-date-worthy guy could adjust was a little hard for Paige to imagine. She was still grappling with it herself. And she knew that no matter how hard they tried to hide it, Piper and Phoebe were grappling with her as well.

It wasn't as if they hadn't had enough to deal with before they came across her—their surprise half sister. They had just lost Prue, the oldest Halliwell sister, in a terrible battle with the source of all evil. Grieving, angry, mournful, and in pain, they discovered there was another Halliwell witch out there. Paige.

After some adjusting—okay, a lot of adjusting—Paige had become an official member of the Halliwell family. She moved into Halliwell Manor—reluctantly at first—and now felt it was her home. And she loved her new sisters, even if they still took some getting used to. She felt more comfortable with Phoebe, who seemed to have had her share of wild days in her not-so-distant past. That was something Paige could definitely relate to. Piper was a bit more mature and responsible.

Or maybe that's just how big sisters act, Paige mused. Paige had grown up as an only child. So dealing with siblings was a new experience.

What was hardest, and what Paige had the most trouble expressing to her sisters, was the pressure she felt to live up to Prue. Not just as a sister—she knew that Piper and Phoebe would never get over their loss. It was her role as a Charmed One. Prue had been a very powerful witch, even more advanced than Piper and Phoebe. Paige had so much catching up to do!

And the Power of Three was based on their being in synch with one another. Really connected. Piper, Prue, and Phoebe had grown up together, had lived in this house together, and then had discovered and developed their powers together. Now Paige had to jump in like an understudy in a play suddenly having to go on for the star at a moment's notice.

Well, one way to deal with that was through preparation. Piper was always on her case about studying. Alone time in the attic with Book of Shadows would keep Paige a few steps ahead of the game.

"But first," Paige announced to the empty house, "more fuel."

Paige padded into the kitchen and poured herself a second cup of coffee. She leaned against the kitchen counter, enjoying the quiet. A tranquil moment was hard to come by for the Charmed Ones. Demons seemed to lurk everywhere—and popped up out of nowhere without warning. Another serious date disaster. And if there wasn't a supernatural threat, being surrounded by exuberant sisters and their mates was noisy. The Halliwells and their significant others took up space.

Still, she thought, starting up the stairs, *it's nice to be part of something*. Not just part of a family again—Paige had lost her adoptive parents in a car accident—but part of something larger. A destiny.

Half of her was excited, exhilarated. But the other half? She shook her head with a rueful grin. *Well, that's why long bubble baths, aspirin, and chocolate were invented, isn't it?*

Paige opened the door to the attic and stepped inside. Unlike other attics, this one wasn't dark and dusty. *Well, not too dusty,* Paige thought as she spotted the motes of dust swirling in the streaming sunlight. It was filled with the usual clutter—abandoned furniture, trunks of old clothes, and long-forgotten souvenirs—but this attic was also a place of magic.

Magic was a 24/7 event in the Halliwell household, taking place in all zip codes, but it often led them up to the attic. This was where they kept Book of Shadows, sort of the how-to guide for witches. It was also where Piper and Phoebe had come into their powers—and introduced Paige to hers.

Paige gazed down at the thick book. Book of Shadows held their past, their present, and possibly their future—or, more accurately, the clues to help ensure they *had* a future. Generations of Halliwell witches wrote down spells of all kinds, along with recipes for potions, protections, charms, and amulets. It also served as a dictionary of the demon world: drawings of twisted creatures of darkness, descriptions of their habitats, weapons, and feeding habits, which, more often than not, included witches.

Paige gave an involuntary shudder. Sometimes,

when she was feeling particularly alone and vulnerable in the wee hours of the morning, she scared herself imagining that the drawings had come to life and were creeping out from between the pages. Then she'd have to get up and calm herself with a mug of herbal tea and by reminding herself that the book existed to protect her. Those creatures were trapped inside Book of Shadows forever. It was there to teach her how to vanquish them.

But there were some pages Paige could look at for hours. One early Halliwell, back in the eighteenth century and obviously in love, had written a ritual for a handfasting, or marriage ceremony, decorated with pressed flowers and delicate watercolors. Another later set of pages describing herbs and their uses included beautiful, intricate drawings of plants. The entries reflected the personalities of the witches who wrote them. Some were pensive, some were joyful, some had funny drawings; all crackled with energy, now that Paige understood how to sense it.

Slowly working her way through the book, Paige came to a page she had never seen. Her brown eyes widened.

"Shape-shifting," she murmured. She felt her heart flutter. *My orbing ability is kiddie stuff compared to this.* She reviewed the entry. It described a magical way to change form—how cool was that! *If I could turn myself into something else,*

Paige thought with rising excitement, *that would be an amazing power. And I'd have a power none of the others have—and one that Prue didn't have either. Something completely my own.*

Paige was half Whitelighter, so she and Leo shared the ability to orb. This power would set her apart from the others.

And one I learned all by myself. Then Piper would realize I do have initiative and take my destiny seriously, Paige thought, recalling a recent argument she'd had with the oldest Halliwell sister. Being able to shape-shift could also round things out in the demon fighting—and end the unfavorable comparisons with Prue.

Paige stopped her mile-a-minute brain for a moment, knowing she wasn't being completely fair. *Okay, so maybe Piper and Phoebe aren't actually comparing me to Prue,* she admitted. *Maybe I'm the one making the judgments. But still . . .*

"Shape-shifting." Paige ran her finger along the page, tingling with anticipation. *To become something I'm not. I could be a bird, or a chair—.* Her nose crinkled. *Well, maybe not a chair.* She giggled at the silly idea.

She read through the spell's instructions. This was a spell for turning into an animal. Whoever had written down the spell advised a witch to choose an animal she easily identified with to start. Eventually, she should be able to shape-shift into all sorts of creatures.

Paige was surprised that so few ingredients

were needed. Flames for transformation. Paige glanced around the attic. *Got plenty of candles— that should do.* She looked at the list again. Comfrey and nettles in an infusion, cinnamon sticks to burn. *Those shouldn't be hard to find in Piper's well-stocked kitchen.*

Paige bounded down the stairs to the kitchen, her mind racing the whole time. "What should I become?" she murmured, rummaging through the cupboards. She grabbed the jar of cinnamon sticks and placed it on the counter.

"Comfrey and nettles," she muttered as she moved along the row of cupboards, opening each as she went. "If I were comfrey and nettles, where would I be?" *I suppose once I get really good at shape-shifting, I could turn myself into comfrey and nettles and find out!* Paige giggled again. She felt practically giddy with anticipation.

She loved magic. The saving of innocents was satisfying and important. Wanting to help others was why she had become a social worker. And the empowerment factor—to be truly connected to the unseen forces of the universe and to feel that coursing through her body as she worked magic—well, that was off the charts. The adventure, the constant discovery, the venturing into the unknown. There was nothing like it.

Paige put on a kettle to boil as she continued to hunt for the comfrey and nettles. "There you are," she cried, grabbing a plastic bag labeled NETTLES. She glanced around the kitchen, trying to figure out what comfrey was and where Piper would store it. "Oh, wait a sec. . . ." Her face brightened as she remembered Piper's stash of teas.

She opened the wooden cabinet. "And there *you* are!" she told the box of comfrey tea leaves. The teakettle whistled on the stove behind her. "Perfect timing!"

Paige chose a ceramic bowl and placed it on the counter. She shook some of the nettles into the bowl, tossed in a handful of comfrey, and then poured the boiling water over them.

"Clean as you go," she reminded herself, repeating Piper's mantra. She resealed the comfrey and the nettles and put them back in their spots. She laid her hands on either side of the bowl. It was hot, but not too hot to carry. She was eager to get started. Tucking the jar of cinnamon sticks under her arm, she gripped the bowl tightly, then slowly, carefully, made it back up to the attic.

Paige's nose crinkled. The nettles and comfrey created quite an earthy smell. She hoped she didn't have to drink the pungent mixture!

She placed the bowl on the floor in the center of the room and went back to the lectern to read the spell more carefully. *Good. No ingesting.* She just had to anoint her forehead, her hands, and her feet with the infusion. *Oops. Which means I should take off my shoes!*

Paige kicked off her clogs and pulled off her

socks. "Okay, now what?" she said, glancing down at the book. Candles. Right. And something to burn the cinnamon stick in so that she didn't burn down the attic.

Paige put the pure white candle behind the bowl of steeping herbs and the cinnamon stick right in front of the candle. She read the incantation over and over, so that she was confident that she had it committed to memory. *Ready to rock and roll!*

Paige knelt in front of her spell fixings and focused on the animal she wanted to be. *Hmm.* Paige sank back onto her heels and let her mind drift. The image of a cat popped into her head. Made sense—Paige loved cats. There was something about their grace she admired. Their independence. Their sensuality and playfulness. She even had an old boyfriend who once told her she reminded him of a cat.

"Perfect," Paige declared. She smirked. "Or maybe I should say purr-fect!"

She was ready. She lit a match and held it a few inches from the wick of the candle. Little butterflies did a tango in her tummy. This was a big step—a major spell attempted on her own.

"Go for it," she ordered herself. She held the burning match to the candlewick and watched it whoosh into flame. No backing out now. She'd begun.

Paige focused her brown eyes on the candle flame. The spell had said to concentrate on the animal she wanted to become while drawing on the transforming energy of fire. She allowed the image of a cat to form in her mind, never letting her eyes waver. Think of the animal's qualities, and then sense those qualities in yourself, the spell had instructed.

The flame flickered and danced. Paige dipped her fingers in the comfrey and nettle infusion and dabbed her forehead, the palms of her hands, and then the tops of her feet. Next she held the cinnamon stick into the flame as she recited the incantation from Book of Shadows:

"I take what I am
Turn it into what I will be.
Animal Power, Animal Me,
Animal Energy, Animal Shape,
Animal Form my body to take."

Once the cinnamon stick began to smolder, she placed it on the small plate beside the candle. Her voice lowered to a whisper. "I am a cat. I am a cat." She repeated the words over and over, her eyes fixed on the tiny blue center at the very heart of the candle flame. She could sense power building within her, and her words went from barely audible to a strong and loud chant. Her body shook, and her hair rose with static electricity. But she never shifted her focus from the candle and never lost the solid image of herself looking out at the world through a cat's eyes.

As her chanting grew to a crescendo the flickering candle flame burst into a six-foot inferno, then instantly blew itself out. At the same moment, Paige let out a wild howl—a sound that shocked her attention away from the candle and the spell.

"Was that me?" Paige wondered out loud.

But what she heard was "Mrrrowr?"

Paige stared down at paws. *Her* paws! She bounded over to the floor-length mirror and gazed at her reflection in astonishment.

She was a cat!

Chapter

2

"I did it!" Paige exclaimed.

She jumped when she heard that weird and unfamiliar "Mrrrowr" again instead of her own voice.

There, in the mirror in front of her, was a small sleek cat. Her fur was the same deep rich brown as her hair. The tips of her ears and her nose were pure black. Her brown eyes were perfectly round, and no matter how deeply she gazed into them, Paige could not detect any sign of her human self.

"It really worked." Paige arched her furred back. *Mmm, that feels good. No wonder cats do it so often.* Next she flexed her front paws so that each little claw popped out. *Awesome. In total working order.*

Concentrating hard, she flicked her tail. The movement startled her, and she leaped up and reached around to bat at the silvery tip. *Look at me! I'm a cat chasing my tail! How goofy can I get?* Paige giggled. Only she didn't make any sound—just felt a slight shiver through her body. *I never have seen a cat laugh,* Paige realized. *I wonder if they have a sense of humor.*

Paige stepped carefully around the room, adjusting to her new four-footed gait. The floor felt spongy under her footpads. She lifted up a front leg. "These are definitely more comfortable than spiked heels," she told her paw.

All of Paige's senses seemed heightened. Her whiskers tingled with the mingling scents of the herbs from the spell, the furniture polish Piper used on some of the woodwork, and the coffee in her mug on the table. Paige padded over to the coffee mug and poked her head over the edge, and she immediately pulled it back out again. Her favorite addiction—caffeine—didn't seem at all enticing now that she was a cat. *Now that's a transformation! Me not liking coffee? Yowza.*

Ooh, but that dust bunny looks like fun. Paige the cat crouched low, then pounced. The dust bunny swirled just out of reach, but Paige didn't care. The thrill was in the chase, the hunt. She was about to pounce again when the warm patch of light streaming through the window made her flop over. *Mmm.* She rolled around, feeling the warming rays heat her fur. The floor was nice and cozy underneath her. Every muscle felt yummy in the square patch of sun.

A soft breeze in the drafty attic sent the dust bunny skittering past her again, but now that she was all comfy in her sun patch, Paige the cat just blinked sleepily at it. She yawned. *Live and let live*, she thought. *After all, what did that dust bunny ever do to me?*

A strange rumbling sound brought her to her feet. *What was that?* It stopped as suddenly as it had started. *As a matter of fact*, she realized, *it stopped as soon as I got nervous.* Then it dawned on her. . . . *Could that have been me? Purring?* She was glad no one had been there to see her scaring herself.

And, she thought as she stretched her front legs up and dug her claws into the upholstered chair in the corner, *I'm also glad no one is here to see me do this, either!* She worked her sharp claws in and out of the fabric, enjoying the stretch.

A door downstairs banged. "You are so going to pay for that," Paige heard Phoebe say, laughing.

"We'll see about that!" Cole countered.

"This I gotta see," Leo teased them.

"Really?" Piper said, laughing. "This is a contest I definitely want no part of!"

Uh-oh. Paige no longer had the house to herself. Her extended family was home.

And I definitely do not want them to see me like this! Paige knew her new skill would go over much better if she demonstrated it from human form, not spring it on them as a cat. Her sisters were pretty anti-unauthorized magic using, especially Piper. Paige was psyched thinking about showing them, though. She just had to find the right approach. *I could even ask permission before I do it,* she decided. But for now, it was time to turn back into Paige.

Just one problem, she thought, her round brown eyes squinting up at the lectern that held Book of Shadows. *How exactly do I do that?*

If she could have, Paige would have kicked herself—with all four feet. *Why didn't I read through the entire spell?* Then a new problem occurred to her. *How will I say an incantation when all that comes out of my mouth are variations of "meow?"*

Still, there must be something I can do. Paige leaped up onto the lectern and stared down at Book of Shadows. It was still open to the transformation spell. The spell definitely continued onto the next page. *It might even go on for pages after that,* Paige realized.

Paige tried to get the thick paper to turn with her paw. She couldn't get the proper grip. *Life is hard without thumbs!*

Now what?

Paige jumped down from the lectern and dashed to the open door. Her hearing was enhanced in this form. She could hear every nauseating sweet-nothing Cole whispered to Phoebe.

Glad I missed brunch. If Cole had been acting like that through the entire meal, I would have gagged on my latte.

She forced herself to take stock of her situation. Despite all the warnings not to, Paige had performed some pretty powerful magic unsupervised. To make it worse, she had been careless, so she couldn't undo what she had done.

It didn't make any sense. Surely the person who wrote the spell would have realized that it was impossible to turn the pages of the book once a witch was in animal form. *Then again,* Paige thought glumly, *the witch writing the spell probably assumed anyone trying out a new spell would read the whole thing through before making an attempt.* She could just hear Piper's lecture now. The worst part was, Piper would be completely, totally right.

There was no time left to figure it out for herself. Her sisters were bound to start worrying about what had happened to her. She didn't want them to set off on a wild-goose chase trying to track her down, especially since she was right here—their new pet. Which she really did not want to become a permanent state of affairs.

As much as she hated to admit it, it was time to let the cat out of the bag. In a manner of speaking.

Paige decided she'd try to catch Phoebe alone. She was pretty sure she could count on Phoebe to be fairly understanding about this kind of thing. Phoebe wasn't big on keeping things from Piper, but at least she could turn Paige back into Paige—and help her figure out a way to confess in the least-painful way possible.

Paige poked her head out the door again. It sounded as if they were all still in the living room.

Paige crept downstairs. She never noticed before how far apart the steps were. Of course, her legs were a lot shorter now that she had four of them. The good news was that paws were much quieter to sneak around on than high heels. She glided silently into the living room and slipped behind a large potted fern.

Leo and Piper were sprawled together on the sofa, sharing the Sunday paper. Vegging out was definitely on their agenda.

Cole stood and stretched. "Time for some training," he declared.

"After that heavy meal?" Phoebe protested.

"You've had plenty of time to digest," Cole countered. "We have to keep you in shape."

"I thought you liked my shape," Phoebe quipped.

"Now you're just trying to distract me," Cole said, grabbing Phoebe's hand and giving it a little tug to get her to stand.

Phoebe reluctantly rose to her feet. "Okay, you win." They headed for the basement.

Paige had to force herself to not meow in frustration. Why couldn't Phoebe decide to change her clothes or go to the bathroom? Now Paige had no idea when she'd get Phoebe alone.

What a cozy scene, Paige thought as she tucked

her tail up under her chin. Leo lay full-length on the couch, his feet in Piper's lap. Piper leaned into the back of the billowy sofa cushions, her feet up on a chair in front of her. *And me, jungle kitty, peering through the leaves just waiting to pounce.* Paige's tail whipped back and forth, on alert for any chance she'd have to get to Phoebe.

After about an hour Paige's ears twitched. *Aha! Could this be it?* She heard footsteps coming up the stairs. She readied her body to move. The door to the basement swung open, and Cole emerged, sweaty and bare-chested.

"Your sister's getting a little too good," Cole told Piper, laughing. "I called uncle. Time to hit the showers."

"Don't mess with the Halliwell sisters," Piper said with a grin. "We're tougher than we look."

"I'll second that," Leo added.

Cole headed toward the stairs. Paige stealthily made her way out from behind the plant, under the couch, resisting the temptation to tug at the fringe on the rug with her teeth, and got to the basement door. She dashed down the stairs.

Just as Phoebe ran up them.

"Agh!" Phoebe shrieked as Paige tangled up in her sister's feet.

Paige flipped over but managed to remain upright. *So the rumors are true*, Paige thought. *Cats really do land on their feet.*

Phoebe stumbled, caught herself, and instantly took a fighting stance on the steps. Her head whipped around. "Okay, I know you're here," she called out. "What are you—an invisible demon?"

"I'm not a demon," Paige assured her sister.

Phoebe's eyes landed on Paige. A confused smile spread across her face.

"See?" Paige said. "It's just me down here."

Phoebe scooped up Paige into her arms. "Well, hello, kitty. How'd you get into the house?"

Oh, no. Paige had assumed that Phoebe would know her in an instant. She hadn't counted on being mistaken for a real cat. How could she get Phoebe to understand the situation?

Piper peeked down into the basement. "Everything okay down here?" she asked.

"Piper! Look what I found." Phoebe charged up the stairs with Paige cradled in her arms.

Paige squirmed, trying to get away. "No!" she protested. "This wasn't the plan." But all that came out was an indignant meow.

"Whose cat is that?" Piper asked.

"I don't know. I tripped over her in the basement," Phoebe explained.

"Okay, I'm totally busted," Paige said. "It's me."

Only her sisters didn't understand her. *This is going to be harder than I thought*, Piper realized with alarm.

"That scream we heard was Phoebe meeting

her new friend," Piper told Leo and Cole, who'd returned to the living room upon hearing Phoebe's shriek.

Phoebe scratched Paige under the chin. "She's so sweet."

Piper raised an eyebrow. "Phoebe," she said. Paige heard the warning tone in her voice.

"What?" Phoebe asked.

"You have that look," Piper said.

"What look?" Phoebe said innocently. She rubbed her face against Paige's fur. Paige could tell Phoebe was avoiding Piper's eyes.

Piper crossed her arms over her chest. "The can't-we-keep-her look."

Phoebe cuddled Paige in the crook of her arm and scratched her fluffy belly. "Well, can't we?" Phoebe said with a grin.

"No," Piper said firmly.

"Why not?" Phoebe asked.

"Yeah, why not?" Paige demanded. She'd like having a cat around the house. It fit in with the whole witch thing. *Oh, wait a sec,* she thought. *A cat other than me, I mean.*

Piper shook her head. "All we need is a cat scratching up the furniture and knocking things over while Paige explodes things in an attempt to figure out her powers."

"Hey, I'm getting a lot better," Paige meowed at Piper. "And don't tell me you didn't make any mistakes when you were first getting your powers under control."

"At least Paige was housebroken," Phoebe quipped.

"Barely," Piper replied with a grin.

"What?" Paige's fur bristled.

Phoebe laughed and pet Paige between the ears. "I don't think kitty here likes what you're saying."

"Great. Another opinion to deal with. See? We already have too many cooks in this broth."

"How'd she get in here?" Leo asked. "We have to be careful, you know."

"Do you think this cute little thing is a demon?" Phoebe scoffed.

"You never know," Leo pointed out. "Some demons can be very appealing until they reveal themselves."

"You should know that, Phoebe," Cole teased. "You thought I was pretty irresistible even when I was still a demon."

Phoebe rolled her eyes. "Ha-ha. Don't remind me."

Cole took Paige from Phoebe and gazed into her eyes, letting her back paws dangle.

"It's me in here, Cole," Paige meowed plaintively.

Cole tucked Paige into the crook of his arm. "Nah. She's just a cat," he declared. "We should check to see if we've got a hole somewhere. Don't want to discover a rat or a raccoon has made a nest in this old house."

"Cole, why don't you drop off our intruder at

the animal shelter," Piper instructed. "I don't trust Phoebe to do it."

"Hey!" Phoebe protested.

"Puh-lese," Piper said. "You'd probably come home with several more little fur balls."

Phoebe threw up her hands. "Guilty as charged. What can I say. I'm a soft touch." She bent over Paige. "Bye, cutie," she said.

"No!" Paige yowled. She dug her claws into Phoebe's red sweater, clinging to her. "You can't give me away!"

Phoebe gave Piper a pleading look. "See? She wants to stay with us."

"Phoebe." Piper's voice was firm.

Phoebe carefully disentangled Paige's claws from her sweater. "Sorry, kitty."

"I'll dig up something to put her in," Leo offered, heading for the kitchen.

"Thanks, hon," Piper said.

"It's me!" Paige protested in a total panic. "Phoebe, Piper. I'm your sister. Paige."

But she knew that all they heard were frantic meows.

"Come on, girl," Cole said, hugging her to his chest. "It won't be so bad. A good-looking kitty like you? You'll find a nice home in no time."

"I have a home!" Paige wailed. "Here!"

"This should work," Leo said, reentering with a Styrofoam cooler and a roll of duct tape. "I punched some holes in the lid. It should work for the short drive over."

Hissing and spitting, Paige fought as hard as she could. But a small cat was no match for a half demon, a Whitelighter, and two determined Halliwells. They placed her in the cooler, Phoebe dropped in a small pillow, then the lid was lowered. Paige heard tape ripping, and she knew she was trapped inside the makeshift carrier.

The holes Leo had cut into the top were too small to see through. She felt herself being lifted and carried out of the house. A few moments later the lurching movement told her that Cole had started up the car. They were on their way to the animal shelter.

Great, Paige thought miserably. *My own sisters just gave me away.*

Chapter
3

Piper placed a big bowl of vegetarian curry on the dining room table, enjoying the scent of the heady spices. "Dinner," she called.

As Leo, Cole, and Phoebe filed into the dining room, Piper ducked back into the kitchen to fetch the tray of condiments—shredded coconut, chutney, raisins, slivered almonds. *Yum*, she thought, eyeing the treats. She placed the tray beside the bowl of fluffy basmati rice. She glanced around the table and noticed the empty chair.

"Paige still hasn't come home?" she asked. Piper had spent most of the afternoon in the kitchen among her pots, pans, and spices. She had been a professional chef before opening the popular club P3 and now just cooked for pleasure. The long, lazy Sunday afternoon had been an ideal time for recreational cooking.

Phoebe poured herself iced tea from the pitcher. "She must have made other plans."

"She could have let us know," Piper grumbled, settling beside Leo at the table. She gave her napkin a quick shake, then smoothed it out on her lap.

She wasn't going to let Paige's inconsiderate behavior irritate her. It had been a lovely, relaxed day. For an entire Sunday, Piper had been almost able to believe that she and Leo were an ordinary couple. That she and her sister were just double-dating and then vegging out at home. Piper intended to keep the mood going for as long as she could. She'd remind Paige to leave notes for them when she got home later. For now, Piper was going to enjoy the exotic meal she had prepared. She smiled. "Dig in, everyone."

Cole loaded up his plate with rice and curry. "I can't believe how hungry I am after that huge brunch."

"Must have been the workout," Phoebe teased. "You burn a lot of calories trying to keep up with me!"

Cole gave her a quick peck on the cheek. "You always put me through my paces."

"If you want, I'll put you through some others after dinner," Phoebe offered, sliding her hand onto his thigh.

"Get a room," Piper quipped. "Oh, right. You already have a room. Right across from ours."

It was nice seeing Phoebe and Cole banter like a regular couple. Piper reached for Leo's hand and gave it a quick squeeze. Nice for all of them to be enjoying a few hours of normalcy— since the Halliwell definition of "normal" was not exactly the same as other people's.

And lately, with Paige added to the mix . . . Piper liked Paige—loved her, even—but she was still getting used to having her around. Still getting to know her. Like with any new roommate, there were always adjustments to make. Then on top of that was the need to get Paige up to speed with the whole Charmed Ones thing. It was a lot of pressure to put on the girl, so new to her powers, but it was necessary. Their very lives—and those of the innocents—depended on it.

Maybe I shouldn't push her so hard, Piper mused, taking a mouthful of the spicy curry. *I should be more patient.* Like tonight. *So she didn't leave a note,* she told herself. *Paige isn't a child. She's a twenty-four-year-old with a job, a car. . . . She even has a basically good head on her shoulders,* Piper admitted.

Still, it would have been nice to have known how many people to cook for. *Well, at least this stuff reheats well. Curry for lunch isn't a bad thing.* She eyed the heaping bowls. *Unless it turns out to be lunch all week.*

After they'd all helped themselves to seconds (and Leo had thirds), Piper announced, "I cooked. You all clean."

Leo pushed his chair away from the table. "I'd say that was a bargain." He piled up the plates and silverware and carried them into the kitchen. Cole and Phoebe gathered the condiment bowls while Piper collected the napkins and followed them into the kitchen. She glanced up at the kitchen clock. "I didn't realize it was already after nine," she said.

"Did Paige mention any plans?" Leo asked, scraping the plates into the garbage disposal.

Piper smiled at him. He knew exactly what she had been thinking. As their Whitelighter, he was dedicated to protecting them, and Paige tended to bring out the big brother in him.

"Someone could have called while we were out," Phoebe suggested. She nibbled the leftover raisins.

"Possible," Leo said. He loaded the dishwasher, then straightened up and looked at Phoebe. "But how many of her friends has she kept up with since moving in here?"

"Not many," Phoebe admitted. "Like, zero many."

"Demon busting can be a full-time job," Cole said sympathetically.

Piper thought back to the morning. Paige had seemed preoccupied. "You know, maybe the reason she didn't come to brunch with us was because she's tired of the whole witch thing." She hated even suggesting it, but it was getting pretty late and there was no sign of their half sister.

Phoebe's jaw dropped. "You think she might have bailed on us?"

Piper shrugged. "That's always a possibility. You remember how resistant I was at times? Well, this is all still pretty new to her. She occasionally freaks out."

"We all occasionally freak out," Phoebe reminded Piper. "But we stick together." She nodded firmly. "And so would Paige."

"Then where is she?" Cole asked quietly.

Phoebe threw up her hands in exasperation. "On a date? At a movie? Jeez. Jump to conclusions, why don't you."

"Didn't you get the feeling something was bothering her this morning?" Piper asked.

"Well, yes," Phoebe admitted reluctantly. "But that doesn't mean she'd abandon the Power of Three. We all have moods," she added pointedly.

"I don't think she's run away," Leo suddenly said. Piper realized that up until now her husband had been quiet on the topic. He looked worried.

"What are you sensing, Leo?" Piper asked him. As a Whitelighter, Leo could usually—though not always—keep track of where his charges were. If he was worried, then there was definitely something to worry about.

"There's something strange about her presence," Leo told them. "Something . . . off." His face turned grim. "As if I'm sensing her through a haze of magic."

"You think a demon got her?" Phoebe asked.

"I can't tell," Leo said. "She doesn't seem to be hurt, though."

"That's a start." Piper automatically went into her calm-in-a-crisis mode. "Let's not panic until we have to," she said, her voice a lot steadier than she felt inside. "Leo, you say she's not hurt?"

Leo shook his head. "Not as far as I can tell."

"Then let's try to find her before that changes," she said with grim determination.

"If a demon nabbed her, there should be some clues," Cole said.

"So, let's make like Nancy Drew," Piper instructed. "Start clue hunting."

As the group scattered Piper took a deep breath, trying to keep the panic down. Being a Charmed One meant living with the perpetual threat of danger. She had trained herself to deal with the fear by facing each problem head-on, one step at a time. Otherwise, she'd wind up overwhelmed, as paralyzed as a demon caught in her freezing spell.

Piper scanned the cheerful kitchen. She'd been there most of the day; she would have noticed something amiss. So where to look?

She heard Phoebe opening and closing doors upstairs, Cole trailing behind her. Leo had gone outside to check around the house. Piper went into the living room, where only a few hours ago she and Leo had lazed around as if nothing were wrong. Piper placed her hands on her hips and shook her head. She knew some of the anger she felt was fueled by guilt. She couldn't believe she had suspected Paige of pulling a vanishing act.

And now I know that Paige is in some sort of magical trouble. She pounded the top of the sofa in frustration. *And I don't know how to help.*

Phoebe bounded back down into the living room. "Her room is the usual disaster area, but I didn't find any signs of a struggle."

"Me either," Cole added, coming up behind her.

Phoebe turned to face him, her face lighting up with hope. "So that means she's probably fine," she said.

Cole's strong, rugged face was grim. "Not necessarily. A solitary witch is an easy target for the right demon," he said. "Paige may not have had the chance to put up a fight."

"Oh, that makes me feel just great," Piper said.

Leo strode back into the Manor. "There's nothing unusual outside," he announced.

Piper threw up her hands. "So now what do we do? We have absolutely no clues to go on."

Leo's expression grew thoughtful. "I keep thinking about that cat."

"We have a missing sister, and you're worried about a stray?" Piper demanded.

"It's something to go on," Leo explained. "Maybe a demon left something open—just long enough for that cat to sneak inside. Then if the demon shimmered out, the cat was trapped indoors."

"Possible," Piper said. "But that doesn't tell us who has her. Or how to get her back."

Leo crossed to Piper and tried to embrace her, but she shrugged him off. She was too on edge for contact.

"Let's check Book of Shadows," she said to Phoebe. "See if we can find something to at least break through the magic haze that's blocking Leo."

"Good idea," Phoebe agreed.

"Cole and I will try to find the point of entry for the cat. That might tell us something."

Piper led Phoebe up the stairs two at a time. Just a little while ago she was reveling in her so-called normal afternoon. *I have to learn to stop jinxing myself.*

Piper opened the attic door and stepped inside, Phoebe right behind her.

"Well, the book is open," Piper added, approaching the lectern.

"Maybe it's a message," Phoebe suggested.

"Could be." Piper reached out and touched Book of Shadows lightly. Sometimes the book itself helped the girls by flipping open to just the right spell at the right time. She hoped this would be one of those times. But Piper didn't feel the tingle in her fingertips that signaled a magical indication.

Piper's nose wrinkled, and she glanced

around the attic. "Do you smell something funny?" she asked. She spotted a ceramic bowl in the middle of the floor. "Someone did a spell in here," she surmised. She nodded toward the bowl, the candles and the plate holding a black-ened cinnamon stick.

"The question is, who?" Phoebe said. "Paige or a kidnapper?"

Piper looked back down at the page in front of her. Her eyes widened as the implications made themselves clear. All too clear.

"Oh, it was Paige," she declared. She shook her head, feeling anger rising. "I can't believe it. She is nowhere near experienced enough to be doing spells like this."

"Spells like what?" Phoebe crowded beside Piper to take a look at the spell. "Shape-shifting." She looked puzzled. Piper watched her sister's expression change as she made the connection. She stared at Piper. "That was no ordinary kitty."

"That was our sister." Piper smacked her forehead. "And I insisted we give her away!" She crossed her arms over her chest. "Well, serves her right."

"Piper," Phoebe scolded. Her brown eyes grew serious. "She heard everything you said," she reminded Piper. "About being housebroken . . . ?"

Now Piper felt guilty. But it was Paige's own darn fault. "She shouldn't be fooling around with things she doesn't understand," she said in a huff. "She obviously couldn't figure out how to reverse the spell. It's worse than having a pet. Those messes can be cleaned up with a strong carpet cleaner. Paige's messes are much more complicated."

"Now is not the time to play Bad Cop," Phoebe told Piper, "Now is the time to play Ms. Fix-it." Her forehead crinkled with worry. "So can we? Fix it?"

"Let's see." Piper sighed. She tucked her long brown hair behind her ears and bent over to try to figure out how to undo whatever it was that Paige had done.

A shout from downstairs sent her on full alert. Her head shot back up. "That was Leo."

Piper and Phoebe stared at each other. Another shout brought the sisters out of the attic and down the stairs.

Piper grabbed Phoebe's arm halfway down the flight, her body cold with fear.

Leo lay sprawled on the floor, struggling with a scaly green creature with drooling yellow fangs. Two other black-clad, slimy green figures dodged the energy balls that Cole lobbed as quickly as he could create them.

Piper's heart pounded as she took in the scene. Leo and Cole were battling a trio of demons!

Chapter
4

"Cole, duck!" Phoebe shrieked. She leaped over the stairway banister and landed a powerful kick on the nearest demon's chin. His green scaly head snapped back, and he flew across the room, slamming full force into the wall.

Cole straightened back up. "On your left!" he shouted.

Phoebe held out her palm, concentrated, and formed an energy ball. She lobbed the magical grenade at the next demon. It exploded on impact, taking out the slimy thing.

Good thing they vanish into thin air when that happens, Phoebe thought. *I'd hate to clean up his mess.*

"Phoebe!" Piper screamed.

Glancing around frantically, she saw a demon gripping her sister from behind, pinning back Piper's arms so that she couldn't freeze any of them. Leo was still sprawled on the floor—and two more demons had shimmered in. *Not good.*

The demon she'd sent flying had scrambled back up to his webbed feet, and now Cole was giving the creature serious competition in the hits, punches, and blows department. Phoebe raced to tackle the new demons surrounding her sister. She could see one of them was about to sink his double row of yellow teeth into her trapped sister's shoulder.

"Pick on someone your own size," Phoebe snarled as she grabbed the hungry demon and spun him around. *What a stink! These demons smell worse than they look. And they look bad!* But they fought well—this one blocked each of her blows with practiced moves.

A glowing energy ball zipped past her ear, sizzling her hair. It connected in the center of the crinkled green forehead of the creature she was fighting. He let out an agonized howl, clutching his face, and he shimmered into nothingness.

The other demons instantly shimmered away. The one with the wicked grip on Piper released her so suddenly, she fell over.

"Ow," Piper complained from the floor. "It's not bad enough to be attacked by slime creatures, they have to make me look like a klutz too?" She popped back up again. "Leo!"

"I'm fine," Leo assured Piper. He slid over to lean against the sofa. "Just bruised and winded."

Phoebe tipped up her head to shout out to wherever the demons went. "You'd better run," she yelled. "We kick some serious demon butt, so back off."

Piper sank down beside Leo on the floor and snuggled against him. "I should never allow Sunday brunch to lull me into a false sense of security."

Cole wrapped his strong arms around Phoebe. "How about you? You okay?" he murmured into her ear.

She closed her eyes and allowed herself to feel the safety of his arms. "I'm okay now."

"*For* now, you mean," Piper added dryly. "We didn't vanquish those sketchy dudes. Just scared 'em off."

"So you think they'll come back?" Phoebe said, worried.

"Don't they always?" Piper complained. "I just hope they don't spread the word that we're missing a sister,"

"From just one attack? I doubt it," Cole said.

"Yeah, she could have just been out." Phoebe gave Piper a wry grin. "The Halliwell sisters have been known to go out occasionally."

"We do?" Piper narrowed her eyes. "I vaguely remember having a social life. Still, we'd better get Paige back—and fast."

"Not just for our sake," Phoebe added. "She's been a cat for who knows how long? We have no idea what the long-term effects of that might be. And we're the ones who gave her up."

Piper covered her face with her hands. "Don't

remind me," she said, moaning. She dropped her hands and gave Phoebe a smirk. "Think this will make her catty toward me?"

Phoebe groaned and tossed a sofa cushion at her sister.

"Did you say that Paige is a cat?" Cole asked.

"We'll explain in the car," Phoebe said. She slung her arm through Cole's. "Take us to the place you brought our so-called stray."

"I'll stay here in case anything happens on the home front," Leo offered. "Who knows? She might even find her way back here."

Luckily, Cole had brought Paige to an animal shelter that was open round the clock. Although the adopting hours were nine to five, Phoebe was relieved to see a sign explaining that there was staff on duty all the time.

Cole pulled to a stop in the empty parking lot. Phoebe climbed out of the car. The moment her booted foot hit the pavement, another slimy green creature shimmered in front of her.

Vets aren't the only ones on duty around the clock, she thought grimly. *So are demons.*

"To your left!" Piper ordered from the back-seat window.

Phoebe sidestepped immediately to her left, leaving the way clear for Piper's freezing spell. It caught the demon midsnarl. Piper climbed out of the car as Phoebe took out the creature with an energy ball, shattering him into bits.

Cole leaped out of the car, and Phoebe could

see he was ready for action. Only there wasn't any.

"Just that one guy?" Phoebe said. "Not that I'm disappointed," she added hastily, "I just want to be sure we're not missing anything."

"I know these guys," Cole said. "They often travel alone. They're rogue demons. No allegiances. No alliances."

"That's good, isn't it?" Phoebe asked. "If they don't work together, they'll be easier to vanquish."

"It may buy you some time," Cole agreed. "But they want your powers, just like any other demons. They seek out vulnerable witches like jackals. They'll often go in after an attack to try to scavenge stray magical energy left over from battle."

"Lovely," Piper said, tugging her coat closed against the cool night breeze.

"I think word has spread about Paige being missing," Cole added. "These demons don't like to fight tough battles. They may think you'll be easy targets, if they've heard the news."

Phoebe gritted her teeth. "I just love being the topic of discussion in the demon rumor mill. Can't they talk about someone else for a change?"

"The faster we retrieve Paige, the faster we'll get these green guys off our backs," Piper pointed out. "Let's go."

Phoebe's high-heeled boots clicked loudly in the empty parking lot. Another breeze riffled her dark hair. The bright reception area of the shelter seemed absolutely cheerful compared to the dark night outside.

It was late, and there wasn't much activity. Phoebe, Piper, and Cole stood in a small room with a row of plastic chairs pushed up against the yellow walls. The desk held potted plants and several photographs of happy animals. A woman who looked to be in her twenties, with light brown hair held back in a clip, sat behind the desk, entering data into a computer terminal.

Phoebe rushed up to the desk. "We want our cat back," she blurted.

The young desk clerk stood up, looking startled. "Excuse me? We only place animals during the day."

Piper gave Phoebe a look. Phoebe knew that look. It meant, *Shut up and let me take over.* Phoebe stepped back to allow Piper to approach the desk.

"Our cat isn't a patient here, though I'm sure she'd get great care," Piper said sweetly. "It's just, well . . ." Phoebe could tell Piper was trying to figure out how to explain this without sounding like a total idiot.

I have no trouble sounding like an idiot, Phoebe decided. *It won't be the first time, and unfortunately, it won't be the last.* "My stupid boyfriend got mad at me and brought you my cat," Phoebe said. *There. Make Cole the idiot for a change.*

Cole raised a dark eyebrow at her but went along. "It's just that you let that cat scratch up my expensive rug, and she sheds all over my expensive suits," he said in mock complaint.

Phoebe held up a hand as if to shush him. She kept her eyes on the young woman. "Please, can we just have her back?"

The desk clerk's gaze went from Phoebe to Cole and back again. Phoebe pouted, and Cole looked guilty. They were both hamming it up. Phoebe had to avoid making direct eye contact with her ex-demon boyfriend. She knew he was struggling as hard as she was to not laugh. The situation was so absurd.

If it weren't so serious, she reminded herself.

The desk clerk watched their faces, then smiled. "I'll see what I can do," she whispered.

Phew, Phoebe thought with relief. The woman totally bought it. *Well, it was a lot more believable than explaining we accidentally gave our sister up for pet adoption.*

"What is the animal's name?" the clerk asked, sitting back down in front of the terminal.

"Paige," Phoebe said.

"Kitty," Cole blurted at the same time.

The desk clerk looked confused. "Uh, I call her Kitty," Cole said.

"You just never bonded with her," Phoebe complained.

"I didn't give a name when I dropped her off," Cole said. "I just said she was a stray."

"He's so heartless." Phoebe covered her face

with her hands, playing the drama queen up to the hilt.

"What breed is she?"

"A Halliwell," Piper muttered under her breath. Phoebe shot her a look. Piper returned one that clearly asked how much more absurd this was going to get.

"She's a mixed breed," Phoebe said. She tried to remember what Paige had looked like in cat form. "Dark brown shiny fur," she said.

"That could describe a lot of cats," the desk clerk said doubtfully.

"Can we just go and find her ourselves?" Piper asked, pushing through Cole and Phoebe to get to the desk. "It would be a lot faster."

"That's really against the rules," the clerk said.

Time to pull out the big guns. "If we don't get her back, we're breaking up," Phoebe told Cole dramatically. "I'll never be able to forgive you."

The desk clerk looked stricken by the idea that if Phoebe didn't get her cat back that very minute, Cole was history. Obviously, the clerk did not want to be responsible for a breakup. That was just what Phoebe was counting on.

"Okay," the desk clerk finally agreed. "But only one of you. And since it's after hours, we need to do this quickly."

"The quicker the better," Phoebe said.

The desk clerk checked up and down the hall,

then motioned for Phoebe to follow her. She briskly led Phoebe down a gleaming white corridor. She pulled a set of keys from her pocket and opened a door. Giving the corridor another glance, she nodded, and Phoebe followed her inside.

Phoebe stepped into a room full of animal cages. She noticed that most of the cages were empty.

"We don't have many strays right now," the young woman explained, seeing Phoebe's surprise.

Phoebe nodded distractedly, her eyes scanning the cages. She moved along the row, past a Siamese, a fat tabby, two fluffy gray kittens, a terrier, a dog who was some kind of bizarre mix . . . and that was it.

Phoebe whirled around, her heart hammering in her chest.

"She's not here!" she exclaimed. "She isn't in any of these cages."

The desk clerk frowned. She grabbed a clipboard hanging by the cages and scanned the top sheet of paper. "I see what happened," she told Phoebe. "I'm sorry. Your cat was already adopted."

Chapter 5

Paige's tail flicked nervously. This was not good. It was bad enough that her own sisters had given her away. But how were they possibly going to find her now? If they ever even figured out that she was now a cat. *Now and possibly forever*, she thought dismally. If she could have, she would have cried, only cats didn't seem to produce tears.

"You're just what we needed." A tall African-American man knelt down to Paige and stroked her head. He was the one who adopted her from the animal shelter.

Paige looked up at his smooth dark skin, chiseled features, and neatly trimmed beard highlighting his strong jaw. His dark eyes were slightly almond shaped, with thick lashes. And right now those eyes were gazing deep into Paige's.

This guy must be seriously into pets, Paige thought. *Or maybe . . .* A creepy thought made Paige's fur bristle. *Maybe he knows I'm human in here. Maybe he's some kind of demon.* She had felt a sort of energy from him the moment they locked eyes in the animal shelter.

The guy scooped her up off the floor. "Aw, who's a cute wittly kitty witty?" he crooned.

Ick. Why do people think they need to talk baby talk to animals? It's bad enough when they do it with babies.

Now he was making kissy faces at her.

Did I say "demon"? Make that "dodo."

Paige squirmed out of the guy's arms. She landed with a thud on the floor, then scampered to hide behind the couch. She was on weirdness overload. She needed a minute to think, and this guy's annoying gushing attention wasn't helping.

A moment later two huge brown eyes were staring at hers. "Don't be scared, Bastet," the guy said. "I'm not going to hurt you."

Bastet? What kind of name is that for a cat?

The buzzer rang, and the guy got up from the floor. Paige watched his sneakered feet cross to the door. She noticed his socks didn't match. Come to think of it, neither did his shirt and jacket. He was dressed in serious dweeb duds.

"I'll be right down," he said into the intercom.

Paige crept closer to the edge of the couch. This was good news. He was going out. *That means I'll have the chance to find some way out of here and get myself back to the Manor and fix this whole mess.*

Uh-oh. In a quick move, the guy pulled back the couch, reached down, and swooped up Paige. Before she could howl, scratch, or bite, he had her back in the carrying case he had brought her home in.

Is this guy so cat crazy that he can't stand to go out without me?

Paige peered out of the wire mesh end of the carrying case, wondering where they were going. She was carried downstairs and out to the street.

Two women leaning against a parked car looked up when Paige arrived outside. One was a short, plump woman in about her thirties, with masses of frizzy blond hair piled high on her head. The other was a much younger, petite Asian woman whose braided hair formed a twist at the nape of her neck. Both wore long white dresses with sandals.

"Hi, Tyler," the plump woman greeted him.

"Hi, Marianna," Tyler replied. He nodded at the Asian woman. "Tina."

"You got the cat!" Tina squealed. She poked her finger into the wire mesh of the carrying case.

"Back off," Paige hissed. She nipped Tina's finger. "Don't you know it's impolite to point!"

"Ow!" The woman jumped back. "She bit me."

Tyler laughed sheepishly. "You have to treat

Bastet with respect," he explained apologetically. To Paige, he sounded as if he'd been the one to bite Tina. "She has a mind of her own."

"Thanks for noticing," Paige grumbled. "And don't apologize for me." But she knew that all the three people heard was a disgruntled meow.

And respect? *Do you call all that baby talk treating me with respect?* Then she reminded herself that she was a cat. She'd been known to get a little mushy with pets herself.

Tyler climbed into the backseat of the beat-up Volvo and slid Paige's carrying case in beside him.

Drat. All Paige could see was the back of the driver's seat. *No wonder cats get so annoyed being cooped up in these things.*

Paige sat tensely in her case, wondering where they were taking her. A disconcerting thought occurred to her. *What if Tyler isn't keeping me? He could be giving me to someone else.* Just to make the trail even harder for her sisters to follow—if they figure it out at all.

For much of the drive, the two women chatted nonstop in the front seat. Tyler occasionally offered a comment, but the women often talked right over him. When they did try to include him, there were awkward pauses, and his jokes fell flat. *He may look good,* Paige observed, *but this dude has no social skills.*

Tina spoke up after a long silence. "I wonder what having the cat will do."

"Do you think it will work?" Tyler sounded very uncertain.

"Something is bound to happen," the older woman, Marianna, said. "The cat is an experiment. If nothing happens, we'll try something else."

Paige's cat body tensed. The conversation was now making her nervous. They had some sort of plan in mind, and it seemed to revolve around her.

The car pulled to a stop, and Paige was carried out of the car. She poked her nose through the mesh at the end of the case and peered out.

It was quite late, and the street was deserted. The few working streetlamps gave off a dismal yellow glow. It looked to Paige that they were in some industrial section of town and were heading toward what looked like an abandoned warehouse. This did not make Paige feel better.

Tyler pushed open a heavy steel door, taking care to not bang Paige's carrying case into the doorframe.

The two women followed them in. Paige's cat eyes adjusted easily to the dark. She didn't like what she saw.

The large space was lit only with candles, and burning incense filled the warehouse with acrid smoke. There were about a dozen people in long linen robes drawing strange marks on the floor with chalk. Obviously, some kind of ritual was going to take place here.

A ritual that needs a cat! Paige realized with alarm. The robes, the incense, the pyramid drawing on the floor surrounded by weird symbols— it all added up to an occult gathering. And her presence here tonight meant it must be one that used animals in its spells. That's what they were talking about in the car on the ride over. Paige's tail puffed out, and the fur on her back stood up. She'd heard of some groups that performed animal sacrifices!

Paige let out a yowl and scratched frantically at the seams of the carrying case. It was useless. She couldn't fight plastic.

Her cry got the attention of the group.

A tall skinny young man with long stringy hair bent down and peered into the carrying case. "Tyler, great, you brought a cat."

"Not *Tyler*," an older man with thick gray hair admonished the young man. "Osiris. We must use our ceremonial names the moment we enter the sacred space."

The young man looked embarrassed. "You're right, of course, most high priest Talus, human representative of Re."

"And you have worn your shoes into the space," the high priest Talus scolded Tyler. "You must purify. We are almost ready to begin."

Tyler ducked his head, returning to his usual slouching posture, but said nothing. He carried Paige to a corner of the room where several white robes hung on hooks. Large bowls of sea salt sat on the floor beside piles of shoes. Drapes had been hung to create a makeshift changing area.

Tyler set Paige's carrying case on the floor and shoved it up against the wall. He removed his sneakers without bothering to untie them, grabbed a robe, and vanished behind the curtains.

Okay, Paige, she told herself, *get ready for action.* The minute one of them opened the case, she'd make a break for it. *You are not going to wind up a ceremonial sacrifice.*

She kept her eyes trained on the main room, hoping for some clue that would help her save her life. She noticed a group of women clustered in the opposite corner, applying makeup and putting on jewelry. Some even added wigs and elaborate headdresses to their attire. *That must be the women's dressing area,* she guessed.

They look as if they're about to perform in a play, Paige observed. In fact, she got a strong sense that most of the people here *were* playacting. As if they all got together to put on some amateur theatrics. A glimmer of hope allowed her to feel a moment of calm. That could mean that their animal sacrifices would all be make-believe too.

She continued to scope out the territory. The men were mostly bare-chested, with fabric draped and tied around their hips. *Someone should give the majority of these guys the address of a good gym,* she thought. The women were dressed in the same long white tunics that Marianna and Tina wore. The whole scene was all too toga party for Paige's taste. Everyone—men and women—seemed to be seriously into jewelry. Earrings, necklaces, broad beaded collars, and bracelets up and down the arm were everywhere.

The movement of the nearby curtain drew Paige's attention from the center of the room. Tyler emerged from the dressing area. Paige barely recognized him.

He wore a flowing linen tunic over a short, pleated, skirtlike garment. A blue and gold fabric headdress framed his face, emphasizing his strong cheekbones and deep mahogany skin tone. Paige was shocked to see he'd outlined his almond eyes with black liner. A broad gold collar around his neck and several arm cuffs completed the look.

Using a curved blue and gold staff adorned with a carved cobra head to steady himself, he placed one bare foot into a bowl of salt. "With the blessings of Nephthys, remove my impurities, so that I may be worthy of these rites."

He did the same thing with his other foot, repeating the chant. He slid his feet into leather sandals. Kneeling down, he went through the whole ritual for each hand.

If I had to do that every time I got ready for an event, Paige mused, *I'd never get out of the house.*

In fact, Paige realized, everyone chanted before they did anything. Entering the main space required a chant, lighting a candle required a set of words, greeting one another had a ritual ring to it.

"Hail, fiery one," she heard over and over again. "Greetings, soft and swift traveler," was the usual reply.

Jeez. They even have secret handshakes, Paige noticed. *How lame can you get?* Paige had always suspected that some of the so-called occult groups relied on all these formal trappings in place of having any actual magical ability. All form and no function. Still, she shouldn't get too complacent. Just because they were frauds didn't mean they couldn't or wouldn't harm her.

Tyler opened her carrying case, but before she could do anything, he slipped a collar over her head. "Wh-What?" she sputtered. She didn't care that the collar was studded with semiprecious gems. She was still on a *leash*! How humiliating!

She tugged away from him, putting all her weight behind her resistance. But she was a small cat, and he was a big man. No contest.

"Don't be that way, Bastet," he crooned. "You're the most important one here."

"You got that right," Paige snapped. "I'm the only one with any actual magical power. But do I get any respect? No."

"I don't think your cat is very happy," Talus said with a smirk.

"Oh, she's just talkative," Tyler assured the older man.

Tyler is a lot more sure of himself in costume, Paige noted. Even his walk was different; the slouching, slumping dweeb with a pretty face was gone. Tyler—in Osiris mode—carried himself with strength and grace. He even seemed taller.

A gong sounded, making Paige jump. She was as skittish as a, well, as a cat. Her nerves were about to give out. Obviously, whatever was going to happen was about to happen.

Everyone in the room gathered into a circle in the center. Tyler handed Paige's leash to Marianna, then strode to the far end of the room.

"Hey!" Paige's head whipped around. She didn't want to be left in the hands of a stranger. Tyler was bad enough.

A gong sounded again, and Tyler sat on what appeared to be a gold throne. On one side of the enormous stately chair was a miniature throne just like it; on the other side was a table holding a large platter covered with a cloth.

Tyler stamped his blue and gold staff on the floor three times. The group began a low chant. "We honor thee as your disciples, thrice-great god Thoth, god of knowledge, inventor of *heka*, the magic of the word."

Marianna tugged on Paige's leash, forcing her to march along as the group paraded in an intricate pattern.

"Watch where you're going," Paige hissed as she ducked out of the way of several pairs of sandled feet. Finally, after they made about a dozen turns around the room, Tyler banged his staff on the floor again and stood up. Everyone stopped.

"I am Osiris, lord of the underworld," Tyler declared. His voice resonated richly in the vast room.

"I am Re, the sun god," Talus answered from the opposite side of the warehouse.

The two men made their way through the group toward each other. When they met in the middle of the room, Talus/Re embraced Tyler/Osiris, then released him. Each man placed a hand on the other's shoulder.

"We are twin souls," Tyler said.

"The journey will be completed safely," Talus replied. "The day will dawn again."

"The night will guard the sleeping souls."

Talus and Tyler continued their formal call-and-response routine. It seemed as if their little scene would never end.

Ho hum. Paige lay down at Marianna's feet. This was so dull she almost wished they'd hurry up and sacrifice her. She was about to die of boredom, anyway.

Tyler and Talus circled each other slowly—oh so slowly, Paige noted. *Can't someone hit fast forward?* Finally, after more pompous phrasemaking, Tyler returned to his place at the throne.

He tapped the staff three times, and Marianna jerked Paige's leash again.

"Time for another round of square dancing," Paige commented. No one heard her sarcastic meows over the chanting.

The group moved in a new pattern, though not any more skillfully than before. There were a lot of people with two left feet in this crew, and if Paige was stepped on one more time, she wouldn't be held responsible for the ankle biting that would ensue!

Tyler signaled by stomping his staff again, and the group halted. "We have made the sacred ankh," he declared.

Paige peered along the rows and saw that he was right. Somehow the group of klutzes had managed to arrange themselves in the shape of an ankh, the ancient Egyptian symbol for life.

Tyler held both arms up. "We commune with the ancients, seeking the mystery. We offer ourselves to thee."

Paige's ears twitched at the word "offer." If they were "offering themselves," like Tyler said, then what did they want with her?

Uh-oh. She was about to find out. Tyler held out his hand and Marianna walked Paige over to him. Taking the leash from her, he wrapped it several times around his arm, leaving his hands free. Marianna scurried back to her spot.

Tyler picked something up off the small table. It glinted silver in the candlelight. Paige's fur bristled with alarm. Tyler was now holding a very lethal-looking knife.

"Mrrrwroor!" Paige howled and hissed at Tyler. She batted at him with fully extended claws.

"We honor thee, Bastet," he said, ignoring her struggle. "We offer you all delights."

And I'm one of them? Paige leaned back on her haunches, trying desperately to stay out of Tyler's reach.

Tyler lifted up the platter that lay on the table and held it over his head. "We purify thee." He lowered it, returning it to the table, and passed his hands over it in a ritual gesture.

Tyler kissed the knife and sprinkled it with salt. "We purify thee," he repeated.

Paige's heart thudded in triple time in her furred chest. This was it, the moment of truth. She arched her back and howled.

"Wait!" Paige cried. "You're all into purification! Don't you think I should at least have a cat bath? I didn't take a shower this morning! My fur is all dusty from the attic! Who knows what I might have picked up at the animal shelter?"

"Hold her still," the gray-haired Talus ordered.

For the first time since he'd assumed the role of Osiris, Tyler seemed rattled. He regripped the knife nervously. He whipped off the linen cloth that covered the platter, brought the knife up . . .

. . . and plunged it into the large juicy steak resting on the platter. He sliced off a piece and held it out to Paige.

Huh?

Paige sniffed the meat. She narrowed her eyes and tried to read Tyler's expression. Was the meat poisoned? Drugged?

"Come on, Bastet," Tyler urged. "Eat up."

Paige would have laughed with relief if she could have. Of course! Bastet! That's what Tyler had named her. This group of poseurs was making offerings to *her*.

Now, that's more like it, she thought, daintily taking the steak from Tyler's fingers.

Tyler placed Paige on a blue velvet pillow on the miniature throne beside his. "Bastet, cat goddess. We honor your presence among us."

He fed her some more meat, then sat on his own throne and banged his staff on the floor again.

"Adorn her, to show our love for her."

Two girls crept forward, heads bowed. Each carried an ornately carved box. Tyler popped open the lids and gazed thoughtfully at the glittering jewels piled high inside. He pulled a gold necklace with a heavy red ruby pendant from one of the boxes and hung it around Paige's neck.

As he stroked her fur Paige felt that current of electricity she had when he'd first picked her up at the animal shelter. Was it magic? Or just plain old chemistry?

This Osiris gig really brought out the best in Tyler, she noticed. Once she was human again, though, she'd have to have a serious talk with him about this group of overdone crackpots.

Now that she was no longer in fear of being sacrificed, she could pay closer attention to the proceedings in front of her. From her perch on her doll-size throne, Paige watched the rest of the ceremony. There was a lot more chanting. Some anointing with oils. More incense burning.

She let out a cat yawn, jangling her dangling clip-on earrings. She was loaded down with jewelry. Each time a person passed her little throne, she received a new adornment. In addition to the ruby pendant and earrings, she now sported a small glittering crown, and three more golden chains, and there were several turquoise beads lying at her feet. Er, paws.

Just as Paige was about to fall asleep from the dull monotonous chanting and incense, Tyler stood and lifted her, pillow and all, over his head.

"It is time," he announced. He stepped down from the throne, and carrying Paige on her pillow over his head, he joined the others. She noticed he now had a very strong grip on her. He wasn't taking any chances. They began to march in complex patterns, and this time Tyler led the chants.

"Osiris, Isis, Seth, Horus—keepers of eternal time. We seek to commune with thee," they droned over and over.

After a while Paige began to feel funny. Woozy. And she tingled all over.

Everything grew blurry. Images swirled by

her. Pyramids. Palm trees. Falcon-headed men. Women with lions' bodies.

What was going on? What was happening to her?

"It's almost midnight," Phoebe said.

Piper had phoned Leo from the animal shelter to let him know what was going on. Now she, Phoebe, and Cole were in the car heading for the address the desk clerk had given them.

"I don't care how late it is," Piper snapped from the backseat. "We have to get Paige back, and we have to do it now."

Phoebe raised an eyebrow at her in the rearview mirror.

"Sorry," Piper apologized. "That came out a little harsh."

"No prob," Phoebe said.

Piper went back to gazing out the window, but she wasn't seeing the scenery. She was too wrapped up in her thoughts.

Fine. She admitted it. She was totally, horribly, completely guilt-ridden. She was the one who had insisted they give away Paige. And, yes, Paige may have created this problem herself, but if Piper was a good witch—and more important, a good sister—she would have somehow recognized Paige. *And I would never have made those snippy jokes about her.*

"So we wake up the neighborhood," Piper

said. "We're Charmed Ones. We do what we have to do."

"Piper's right," Cole said. "We need to find Paige and turn her back into herself before any more demons show up. The Power of Three isn't meant to be two women and a cat."

"Okay, this is the place." Phoebe pulled up to a small apartment building in a run-down neighborhood. Liquor stores, check-cashing places, and betting parlors lined the street.

"You guys stay here," Piper said. "Three strangers showing up at midnight might be a little overwhelming."

"Good thinking," Phoebe said.

"We're here as backup if you need us," Cole assured her.

Piper climbed out of the car, hurried up the front steps, and rang the buzzer. She leaned on it hard, knowing full well that this Tyler Carlson person could easily be asleep. But this was an emergency. If she came across as a crazed cat-loving maniac, so be it. She had to set things right.

"Come on, Tyler Carlson," she muttered. "Answer the door."

"He's not there," a voice called up to her.

Piper glanced down. There was a man pulling down the gate of a bookstore just below the stairs.

"What did you say?" Piper asked. She peered

down at the man. He looked about fifty, with a
bulging stomach barely covered by his stained
T-shirt. He wore a little beret, and baggy jeans
over work boots.

"You're looking for Tyler, aren't you?" the
man asked. "Well, he's not home."

"Do you know where he is?" Piper asked,
coming down the stairs.

The man squinted at her, as if he was trying to
decide whether he should tell her or not.

"I was supposed to meet him, but I'm late,"
Piper added.

"He's at the Disciples of Thoth meeting. He
goes every week," the man explained.

Piper was about to ask the man who the
Disciples of Thoth were when she realized that
she'd do better if she pretended she knew
exactly what he was talking about. "I know," she
claimed. "I was supposed to meet him here so
we could go together. It's my first time. I don't
know the address. Do you know where the
meeting is?"

The man eyed her curiously. "You are a new
disciple?"

Whoa. What sort of guy is this Tyler Carlson?
Some kind of cult freak? "Considering it," Piper
said. "Are you a disciple too?"

"I was initiated," the man said proudly.
"When I saw the need, I created another group.
We meet here at my store." The man gestured to
the picture window behind him. Piper now saw

that the bookstore specialized in books on the occult. "When Tyler kept buying all those books on ancient Egypt and Egyptian rituals, I knew the Disciples of Thoth was for him. I introduced him to the group."

"Please tell me where the meeting is," Piper begged in what she hoped was her most persuasive tone. "I don't want to have to wait until the next one. Besides, Tyler will be worried if I don't show up."

The man stroked his chin, then tugged on his beret. "Sure. It's on Belmont and Carlyle. Number fifteen. Don't let the desolation sway you. They're there inside."

"Thank you so much," Piper said.

"Always happy to lead a believer to the true path."

Yeah, whatever. Piper raced back to the car. She gave Phoebe the address, and they drove quickly to the location.

"This Tyler guy is into some weird cult," Piper informed Cole and Phoebe. "They call themselves the Disciples of Thoth."

"Thoth?" Cole repeated. "Sounds familiar."

"Uh-oh," Piper said. "Don't tell me. Thoth is some famous evil demon."

"No," Cole replied. "I think he's an ancient Egyptian god." He twisted around in the front seat to face her squarely. "But I'm pretty sure he's one of the good guys."

"Finally, some good news," Piper murmured.

But she knew nothing would feel right until Paige was back at home—and human.

"That's it!" Piper cried. "Ready or not, Thothites, here we come."

They parked and scrambled out of the car. After the night they'd had so far, Piper was relieved when they made it into the building without attracting attention—demon or human.

Before they even entered the building, Piper could hear chanting. It was some language she didn't recognize. As they opened the heavy door pungent incense hit her hard, making her eyes water. *These Disciples of Thoth don't stint on the aromatherapy,* she thought. Putting a finger to her lips to indicate that Cole and Phoebe should maintain total silence, Piper creaked open the door.

An amazing scene was unfolding in front of her. A group of robe-clad people marched in a strange procession, chanting and swinging bowls of smoldering incense. In the center of the group was an ornately dressed African-American man, holding a cat on a velvet pillow over his head.

A cat she was pretty sure she had seen before.

As Piper stared the handsome bearded man with the cat twirled round and round, the chanting reaching a crescendo.

A brilliant light flashed, blinding Piper momentarily. She heard a shriek, and when she could see again, she gasped.

The man in the headdress and the cat were both gone!

Chapter

6

Phoebe's brown eyes were huge, open nearly as wide as her mouth. She was having trouble processing.

The good-looking young man and cat didn't shimmer away like a demon, didn't orb like a Whitelighter. They disappeared in a poof of smoke. Like in some cheesy Vegas act.

"Wh-What happened?" Piper stammered in front of her.

"Special effects?" Phoebe offered. In all of her experience with magical exits she had never witnessed one quite like that.

"Well, whatever happened, the rest of the gang is as surprised as we are," Cole said.

Her fiancé was right. The ritual they had crashed was now in total chaos. Incense bowls had clattered to the floor, gongs were dropped, and the entire makeshift "temple" buzzed with

the questions, gasps, and astonishment of the
Disciples of Thoth.

"I'd say the ceremonial portion of the proceedings is over," Phoebe declared. "So maybe
they wouldn't mind if we ask a few questions."

"Let's go for it," Piper agreed.

"And I'll check the place for demonic activi-
ties," Cole said.

Phoebe and Piper strode toward a knot of
people. Strange markings on the floor caught
Phoebe's eye. They were obviously magical
symbols, but Phoebe didn't recognize them. She
did recognize the looks of shock and wonder on
the faces around her, though. She'd seen that
expression often enough on her sister Paige's
face when she was first discovering her powers
as a Charmed One.

Paige. Phoebe bit her lip. *If that cat was Paige,
how are we going to get her back now?*

"Excuse me," Phoebe said, tapping a tunic-
clad woman on the shoulder.

The woman turned around.

*Whoa. Someone needs to give this woman some
makeup tips,* Phoebe thought. The woman's blue
eyes were thickly rimmed with black eyeliner,
extending far out to the sides, practically to her
temples. Blue eye shadow had been applied
with a heavy hand. Wisps of light blond hair
snuck out from under a black wig. *This chick has
seen the movie* Cleopatra *too many times,* Phoebe
thought.

Lightbulb moment. She glanced at the group around her. The costumes, the makeup, even the cat—these people had a thing for all things Egypt. Cole was right. There was some kind of Egyptian connection here.

"How did you get in here?" the woman asked Phoebe.

"What just happened?" Phoebe countered, hoping to distract the woman from her question. "It looked amazing."

The woman's expression changed from suspicion to awe. "I know!" She clutched Phoebe's arm. "Can you believe it? Tyler actually managed to join the ancients!"

"What do you mean, 'join the ancients'?" Piper asked.

"Tyler was magnificent," a skinny young man nearby added, joining them. "I always knew he had something special."

"Uh, we always thought so too," Phoebe said, eyeing the scrawny guy's straggly dishwater-blond hair. It was seriously at odds with his eye makeup. "But what exactly did he do?" She hoped they were so stunned by what had happened that they'd be willing to discuss their rituals in front of strangers. Especially if they believed that the strangers were friends of the man in question.

"Oh! Look at poor Tina!" The woman dashed away to comfort a petite Asian woman in the corner, who was rocking back and forth on her heels crying. Nearby two people tended to a gray-haired man who had fainted. *Whatever Tyler did,* Phoebe realized, *it was out of the ordinary.* And he had made Paige a part of it.

"This was big," the scrawny dude murmured beside her.

"What was the ritual for?" Phoebe asked.

"We've been trying to connect with the ancient deities for some time," the guy explained. "Tyler has been designated as priest in the form of Osiris."

"Not that there weren't objections." A plump older woman in another Cleopatra wig joined them. She gave a quick glance to the gray-haired man still lying on the floor. "Johnson had been Osiris but was voted out when there was no magical progress after months."

"But what was he trying to do?" Phoebe insisted, trying to keep them on track. "All rituals have a focus. What was Tyler's? And why did he need a cat?"

"The cat was Tyler's idea," the scrawny man explained. "Since cats were sacred to ancient Egyptians, he thought maybe we would please the deities by including one of their representatives in the ceremony."

"He must have been right!" added the plump woman. "This was the first time this kind of thing worked!"

Or maybe having a witch who can also orb helps things along, Phoebe thought, although she hadn't noticed any of the telltale white lights that usually accompanied orbing. Then again, maybe orbing as a cat was something altogether different.

"But what was he trying to *do*?" Phoebe asked again. She was beginning to feel like a broken record. These people were so stunned by whatever had happened that it was hard to keep them focused. They could barely answer simple, direct questions.

The man shrugged. "I don't know."

Great.

"Our role in the ritual is to help harness the powers of the ancient ones to aid the purposes of the priest," the plump woman explained. "I don't know what Tyler's purpose was."

"To get out of here?" Piper muttered behind Phoebe. "There seems to have been some tension in the group."

The woman gave a dismissive wave. "Oh, Tyler would never want to leave," she protested. "He was more gung ho than any of us. We sometimes had to force him to call it a night. He could have gone on for hours."

The skinny man with them laughed. "I bet Tyler is as surprised as we are. The spells have never worked before."

Just our luck, Phoebe thought grimly. *The one time the rituals of this group of wackos works is the one time my sister has turned herself into a cat.*

Cole came up behind Phoebe and tugged her

elbow. She knew that signal: *Private confab, pronto.*

"Well, uh, good luck with your ceremonies," she told the two disciples. She, Piper, and Cole excused themselves and huddled in a quiet corner.

"Did demons have anything to do with this?" Piper asked.

Cole shook his head. "Not likely. No demonic residue. No signs of evil."

"So we're still minus a sister," Phoebe said. "And we have no idea where she's gone."

"But we know that someone who knows almost nothing about magic somehow made that happen," Piper added.

Phoebe sighed. "And that'll probably be the key to getting her back."

All of Paige's fur stood on end. Not from fear—it was because whatever magic just happened created a lot of static electricity. She could use some serious hair products.

What *did* happen? She and Tyler were alone—and in a new place. It was dark here too, but vacant. No candles, no costumed worshipers. And the place was even larger than the warehouse "temple." The floor was tiled, and Paige's cat night vision could make out huge statues, carved pillars, and wall paintings covering every surface.

Tyler must have transported us to another Disciples of Thoth meeting, Paige thought. She recognized some of the symbols that had been written on the floor in the warehouse on some of the walls here. And the figures in the paintings were dressed like Tyler. But where exactly where they? And how did Tyler do it?

Maybe her first instinct had been right—that the electricity she's sensed between them wasn't just all hormones. *Maybe he does have some kind of power.*

Tyler looked around him, confused. He seemed dazed. "Wh-What happened?" he murmured.

"Well, if you don't know, I certainly can't tell you," Paige responded.

Startled by her meow, Tyler glanced down at her, still sitting on her pillow. "At least I still have you," he told her. As he stroked her head Paige could feel his fingers trembling. He was pretty shook up.

He placed Paige carefully on the floor, then turned in a circle, as if he was trying to take in his new surroundings. "Okay, I managed to transport us somewhere," he said slowly, piecing it together.

Paige heard a slight cracking sound, and then a beam of bright sunlight shone into the dark space. A door must have been opened, because the shaft of light widened, then disappeared again, as if the door was closed behind whoever had entered. Next she heard some shuffling footsteps.

A tall man with a shaved head came into the

area. He wore a linen tunic, plainer than Tyler's, and he didn't wear the jewelry Tyler did. He crossed to each corner of the room—never noticing Paige and Tyler—and lit first a candle, then a stick of incense. Paige could hear him chanting softly as he went about his work. His movements were methodical and sure; he obviously went through this routine every day.

Now that the candles provided more light, Paige could see an enormous statue of a cat at one end of the temple. It was so large that the cat's ears grazed the painted ceiling. Between the paws of the highly decorated statue stood a life-size figure of a woman—with a cat's head. In front of the cat-headed woman was what was obviously an altar—candles, offering bowls, and other tools for rituals sat on the elegant altar cloth. Flanking the altar were two more statues. *Cats again? These people are cat crazy*, Paige thought.

The bald man stopped in front of the cat-woman. Taking a pure white cloth from the altar, he dusted her from head to toe. He removed a headdress made of wilting flowers and replaced it with a fresh one. Kneeling, he poured fresh water from the pitcher he carried into the gleaming golden bowl sitting between the candles on the altar. Paige could hear him murmuring incantations or prayers the whole time. Then he stood, turned around, and gasped.

"What are you doing in here? How did you

get into the innermost shrine?" he demanded of Tyler.

"I . . . uh . . . well . . . ," Tyler stammered.

"The sanctuary entrance is sealed with wax every night," the man said. "I am the only one who breaks the seal every morning!"

"Well, you see . . ."

Paige pawed at Tyler's leg. If he panicked and transported out of there, she didn't want him to forget about her! He picked her up and cradled her in his arms.

"Oh, you are also a devotee of Bastet," the priest said, eyeing Paige.

"Very much so," Tyler replied.

The priest took a few steps closer. Paige could tell he was still suspicious, but seeing her had bought them some time. The priest's eyes narrowed. "You are a foreigner."

"How did you know?" Tyler asked.

Sheesh, Tyler, Paige thought. *Way to be dumb.* If she could have, she would have rolled her eyes. It was kind of obvious that they were from somewhere else. And that this guy didn't take kindly to tourists who trespassed.

"Your beard," the priest said flatly.

Tyler stroked his trim Vandyke. "No one here has a beard?" he asked.

"That is not the sacred beard of kingship," the priest said sharply.

Paige dug a claw into Tyler's wrist. The guy was very bad at reading cues. It was clear to

Paige that the priest wasn't making friendly chitchat and that he didn't like out-of-towners. Yet Tyler seemed oblivious.

"Spy!" the priest shouted. "Are you here as an assassin? Who sent you?"

"No one sent me," Tyler protested. "I'm not here to hurt anyone. I just wanted to—"

"Guards!" the priest shouted. "Guards, we have a spy among us."

The door to the temple opened, and several men carrying spears rushed in.

"Seize him!" The priest pointed at Tyler. "We will show his king what we do to spies."

This is not good! Paige thought. *If they seize Tyler, they seize me, too!* Her fur bristled and her tail thrashed as panic surged through her cat body.

Little white balls of energy erupted around her, as they always did when she orbed. In an instant they were outside the dark temple in pounding hot sunlight.

Paige blinked. *I orbed,* she realized. *I do have powers in this form.* Now her tail flicked with irritation. *I could have orbed myself out of that animal shelter and back home as soon as Cole had dropped me off. This whole stupid episode would already be over. Which means this little adventure is going to end— right now!*

She just hoped Tyler hadn't transported them too far from home. She had never orbed major distances on her own. Judging from that glaring sun, they were somewhere that had much warmer weather than she'd been experiencing at home in San Francisco.

Paige was pretty sure she had orbed them only a few feet, just outside the temple walls. *Make that the enormous temple walls,* she amended. Her eyes traveled up, up, and up the massive walls of the massive building.

An even larger structure caught her eye.

Looming above the temple rooftop was a very familiar monument.

The Sphinx. And it looked a lot newer than it did in the pictures she had seen in her books back home.

Chapter

7

"I did it!" Tyler said, his voice shaking with emotion. "I really, really did it."

The shock must have made his legs weak. Tyler dropped to his knees, staring up at one of the most famous profiles in history.

Paige was struck speechless. Not that she could speak in words, anyway. But she had never imagined that Tyler had the kind of magical power that could send them across the globe—and far, far back in time.

So far back, in fact, that maybe her sisters wouldn't be able to find her. Which meant she'd be a cat forever. And she knew she couldn't orb herself out of this one.

"Listen, you!" Paige swiped Tyler's arm with her paw. "You figure out what you did and reverse it. Right now!"

Startled, Tyler glanced at Paige. Then he

swept her up into his arms. "And it's all thanks to you, Bastet!"

He kissed her nose, then scratched her under her chin. "I couldn't have done it without you." He laughed. "I certainly never have before." He cocked his head to one side. "Then again, I have been studying for some time."

He lowered Paige back to the ground. He stood and held his arms out wide. "It finally paid off," he declared gleefully. "And my wish to be a part of ancient Egypt must have given me the ability to understand the language!" He touched his lips with wonder. "I am speaking ancient Egyptian!"

"I guess it spilled over onto me, too," Paige commented. "Imagine. I'm meowing in a dead language." She didn't feel quite so ecstatic as Tyler over this.

Paige sat back on her haunches. This guy was so proud of himself, he seemed ready to do cartwheels. His exhilaration reminded her of her own, when the high-level shape-shifting spell had worked.

Yeah, and look where that got you, she reminded herself, her whiskers twitching. She hoped Tyler's brand-new spell-casting ability didn't have disastrous consequences.

Still, she knew the sense of accomplishment he was feeling. She'd let him enjoy his moment. But only for a moment.

"I wished I could be in ancient Egypt, and

here I am!" Tyler said, putting his hands on his hips. "Man, I'm good."

This guy jumped from awestruck to arrogant in nothing flat. "Don't you mean, here *we* are?" Paige corrected him. "You're not the only one this wishing spree affected."

"And that was a slick move, wasn't it?" Tyler said to Paige. "Getting us out of the temple like that?"

"Excuse me?"

"It felt different from when I transported us here, though. I guess traveling through time feels different from simply moving from one local location to another."

"Well, duh," Paige said. "Only it wasn't you, it was me!"

Hmm. Maybe it was me during the ritual in San Francisco too. She shook her head. Not a chance. *I never would have wished us into this place. I like the beach as much as the next girl, but this heat is ridiculous.* She felt as if she were going to melt. Well, wearing a fur coat in ninety-degree weather wasn't helping the matter.

Still, Paige suspected that the ritual worked because she had been part of it. She looked at Tyler, wondering if he had some latent magical ability that she—and the ritual—had awakened.

"Isn't it great, Bastet?" He tucked her into the crook of his arm. "I can learn so much more about the magic of Thoth. Of Osiris. Of Isis. I can learn how they really performed the rituals, instead of just trying to guess." He chuckled. "Or maybe they'll learn a thing or two from me!"

Now that the shock had worn off, Paige was able to assess her surroundings. She and Tyler were on a quiet side road. The few people strolling past didn't pay much attention to them, despite the fact that she was a cat loaded down with more jewelry than a starlet and Tyler was wearing eye makeup.

Paige noticed one or two men dressed like Tyler—in a full-length tunic over a short, pleated linen kilt—but most were more simply dressed. None wore the blue and gold headdress or carried the painted cobra staff. All nodded deferentially when they passed.

They must think he's important or royalty, she realized. *That's why they're leaving us alone. And if he's royalty, it would make sense that his cat would be all dressed up too.*

At least we won't attract too much attention, she thought with relief. *That should buy us enough undisturbed time to figure out what to do.*

"Where should we go first?" Tyler muttered.

"How about home!" Paige suggested.

"I'd love to get to the pyramids at Giza." He shaded his eyes and gazed over at the Sphinx. "But it looks like that's a few miles away."

Paige could feel the excitement radiating from him. He was practically giddy.

Paige let out a frustrated meow. If only she could talk to Tyler. She didn't just want to explain her situation, she also felt as if she needed to warn him. He was too thrilled to realize that there may be danger here. Didn't that priest accuse him of being a spy or an assassin? For that kind of instant suspicion, there must be trouble brewing.

"Of course, I could always transport us over to Giza magically. Now that my powers have kicked in." Tyler's chest puffed out a bit as he swelled with pride. "Yow!" he yelped. "Bastet, why did you do that?" Tyler rubbed the spot on his ankle that Paige had nipped.

That's all I need. An overly cocky novice thinking he rocks in the spell department.

Hmm. Her whiskers twitched. Her assessment of Tyler—who did that remind her of? *Me! It was precisely that attitude that got me into this predicament.*

This was even more worrisome to her than Tyler's blind excitement. *He's going to think he can get himself out of trouble even when he can't. And in this cat form I don't know how much I can do to help.*

"I'll get myself oriented first," Tyler decided. "Then I'll use my magic to take us wherever we want to go."

"There's only one place I want to go, and that's home!" Paige protested. But Tyler wasn't listening. He was too eager to check out their surroundings.

They rounded the corner, and even Paige could not contain her awe. A bustling ancient town sprawled out in front of the temple.

Mud-brick buildings bleached white by the sun stood close together, creating narrow sandy passages. A few people rode donkeys, large baskets slung on both sides of the animals. Women and men carrying goods to sell at the marketplace walked along the dusty streets. Scattered palm trees offered very little shade in this section of town. Overhead, large birds called to one another, their cries mingling with the sounds of hammers pounding, dogs barking, and children laughing.

Paige finally shared Tyler's wonder. *We are back thousands of years,* she realized, the truth of it finally hitting her. *I don't know how he did it, but he sure did it!*

Everywhere Paige looked, another extraordinary sight greeted her. A group of young boys—none older than twelve—played a game nearby. What was most startling about them was their unusual hairstyle. Each had a shaved head, except for one braid hanging on one side. Paige didn't think the look would catch on—not even among the more hard-core punk types down around Fillmore Street.

"If this is the temple complex," Tyler murmured, "then, if I'm not mistaken, we should be near the craft workshops."

"Whatever you say, buddy," Paige said. "You obviously know more about this place than I do."

Farther down the dusty street, just as Tyler had predicted, several artisans were working in small tented stalls. One was curing leather hides, another was blowing delicate glass beads.

Paige glanced behind her and realized that the impressive building was the front of the temple they had just vacated. Two rows of small sphinx statues lined a formal walkway, leading to a massive gate. Gold-tipped obelisks flanked the gate. *That is one fortified building,* Paige thought. *No wonder the temple priest had been so shocked we had gotten in.*

Tyler carried her through the craft workshops. Some craftspeople worked at tables under canopies; others had whole buildings as shops. Most of the people they passed nodded at Tyler respectfully.

A young woman approached them. "Please," she said, ducking her head. "When you next speak to the gods, ask for blessings for my new child."

"What?" Tyler asked.

The woman looked flustered, then nodded. "Of course." She removed a turquoise bracelet from her arm and slipped it over Paige's head. "Take this offering to Bastet."

"But—"

The woman hurried away and disappeared into one of the small buildings.

"That was weird," Tyler commented.

"Yeah. I've never been into turquoise," Paige said.

"They sense my power." Tyler smiled broadly.

"No, you jerk. They think you're some kind of visiting aristocrat." *Sheesh.*

Tyler glanced at her. "You must be part Siamese," he said. "They're the only breed I've ever known to be so talkative."

"For Bastet," an old man croaked at them. He waved them over to his tent, where he was making gold jewelry. He clipped a scarab earring to one of her ears.

Paige's head tipped toward the ear with the new earring. *Hey! That's heavy!* She'd have to find some way to get rid of it.

"Bastet will protect you," Tyler told the man.

They soon came to a market. Paige would have guessed that even with her eyes closed. All around her merchants shouted out the wares they had for sale and customers haggled for bargains. She and Tyler had to step carefully to avoid being trampled by animals being brought in and to not crash into men and women carrying large ceramic jars and baskets.

"I wish I could get us something to eat," Tyler muttered.

"Oh, right," Paige said, nodding. "We don't have any money." She eyed Tyler's robes. "No pockets in that costume, I'm guessing."

"Let's see. The ancient Egyptians rarely used money. They worked on a barter system," Tyler said thoughtfully. "But we don't have anything to trade. Except . . ." He squinted at Bastet.

"Okay, that's it!" Paige let out a yelp. "If I am given away one more time—"

"Hold still, Bastet," Tyler said in a soothing voice. He removed the heavy scarab earring. Her head felt instantly lighter.

"I don't want to trade away any of the jewelry the Disciples of Thoth gave you, since I'll have to return it. But these new gems . . . You don't mind too much, do you?"

"Not at all," Paige replied. "I think the feeling should return to that ear pretty soon."

"I don't know how much this is worth, but we should definitely barter for some water. You can get dehydrated in this climate really easily."

Tyler approached a stall that had large ceramic jugs standing in rows. "Peace, in peace," he said to the merchant, laying his hand over his chest.

"In peace, traveler," the man answered. "What's your pleasure?"

"Just water," Tyler replied.

"I have beer and palm wine."

"I don't think my cat companion would like either of those," Tyler said.

"Ah, for the cat. I'll see what I can do."

The man disappeared behind the back wall and returned with a bowl filled with water. "Take it as an offering for Bastet," the man said.

Good thing, Paige thought. *When I quit drinking, I never foresaw having this kind of problem getting a nonalcoholic beverage!*

"And for yourself?" the merchant asked Tyler.

"I'll try the beer."

The man gave Tyler a jug and a straw. *Interesting way to knock back a frosty one*, Paige thought, though it was obviously far from frosty—there was certainly no ice at this refreshment stand.

Tyler gave him the scarab. "That will cover it," the man said. "And I'll give you a pouch of water for your cat to take with you."

"Much obliged. Bastet will honor you."

Paige felt much better after lapping up the water. But they still didn't have food, and she was hungry.

She lifted her nose into the air. *Might as well get some mileage out of these heightened senses of a cat*, she figured. Mingled scents tickled her whiskers. Concentrating, she tried to separate out the good smells from the bad. *Aha!* A pronounced fish smell wafted her way. *Delicious!*

"Come on," she told Tyler in an encouraging meow. She leaped from his arms and dashed along the street.

"Bastet!" he called after her. She could hear his footsteps behind her. Good. He was keeping up with her.

Paige took a sharp turn. Following her nose, she padded up thick mud steps to the roof of a house. "Bingo!"

Stacks of fish lay drying in the sun. A servant

waved a fan, trying to keep the flies off. She never noticed Paige creep forward and drag a fish from its tray backward to Tyler, who had stopped midway up the stairs.

"Clever girl!" Tyler whispered.

"You don't know the half of it." Paige snuck back to the tray and snagged another fish. Soon she had a pile of fish at Tyler's feet.

"What would I do without you?" Tyler said, petting her.

"Good question."

They ate their snack, leaving them both greasy from fish oil. Where could they wash off? Tyler didn't want to use the water in the pouch—it was far too precious.

"We can wash our hands—or paws—in the Nile!" Tyler suggested. He stood and shut his eyes, making Paige wonder what he was doing.

"Concentrate," he instructed himself. "Nile, show thyself to me."

Oh, great. Now he thinks he can use magic to figure out which way to go. Typical guy. Why can't he just ask for directions?

Paige climbed back up to the rooftop. This time the servant spotted her. The woman smiled at her. "Sacred one, have you come to bless our food?"

"Sure, why not," Paige said. She crossed to the woman, who pet her and gave her another fish treat.

Paige hopped up onto the side wall.

Squinting in the setting sun, she craned her neck to try to see the mighty river.

"You look toward the Nile?" the servant asked. "Is that where the good fishing is?"

That answers that, Paige thought. *Nile, here we come.*

She jumped back down and hurried over to Tyler. He still stood there, communing with the Nile flow or something.

"Come on, hotshot," Paige meowed at him. "I've got the map."

"Bastet?" Tyler's eyes popped open.

Paige started down the stairs. She knew he'd follow her. She was right.

"You haven't steered me wrong so far," Tyler said. He bounded down the stairs after her.

Very quickly, they arrived at the quayside on the banks of the Nile. Once again, the scene before her took Paige's breath away.

The sparkling blue Nile was filled with water traffic. Small fishing boats made of bound reeds floated by, their owners using poles to guide them. Larger boats were being unloaded up and down the docks, the workers carrying sacks of grain and wheat to bring to the market. Other goods were being carted away from the harbor as well: enormous stones for building, crates of ducks. Scavenging animals prowled the waterside, and pyramids rose majestically across the wide river.

"This was exactly the direction I sensed,"

Tyler claimed. "And did you see how everyone is treating me? They can tell. My powers are growing. Who else could have traveled back in time like this? This is only the beginning. . . ."

Blah-blah-blah, Paige thought. She was getting really tired of hearing Tyler boast about his so-called powers.

"I should try something even more grand next. There's no stopping power like mine."

Wanna bet? Paige swerved suddenly and tangled herself up between Tyler's feet.

"Yah!" he shouted as he took a few stumbling steps forward. Then he lurched and tumbled off the dock, landing with a splash in the river.

"You wanted to see the Nile," Paige taunted in her cat voice. "I'd say you've got a close-up view now."

That should teach him. Power? *Sorry, buddy. The only one with power here is this little kitty cat, yours truly.*

Tyler splashed in the water, his long robe billowing around him. He didn't seem in any danger of drowning, however. In fact, he seemed to be having a good time.

Unbelievable. I try to take him down a peg, and he just lands on his feet, like a . . . well, like a cat!

She had to admit Tyler was awfully appealing. His excitement was like a little boy's. The water must feel refreshing on this hot day. And even now he was having fun with this mishap. The Tyler in ancient Egypt was completely different from the awkward and shy Tyler she had met at the animal shelter.

She couldn't help smiling—on the inside. Externally, she made do with a satisfied purr. She had discovered something about purring: It wasn't just an expression of pleasure; it felt good, too!

Then her purr caught in her throat.

A crocodile was heading straight toward Tyler!

Chapter
8

"Tyler! Look out!" Paige shouted. But, of course, all that came out of her mouth was a cat howl.

Paige squeezed her round cat eyes shut tight and tried to orb Tyler out of the river. Nothing happened!

How did I do it from the temple? she wondered. *Figure that out later,* she scolded herself. *You have to do something, now! Before Tyler becomes a croc snack.*

She lifted her front leg, hoping to throw an energy ball. The pads on the underside of her paw tingled, as if they were trying to generate the current of an energy ball, but nothing materialized. Besides, she'd have no aim if she tried to lob the thing. *Grrr! Paws are useless.*

She paced back and forth on the pier. Everyone was busy; no one had noticed Tyler, and they sure weren't going to notice her. She had to help him. She had knocked him into the Nile. If that crocodile gobbled him up, it would be her fault.

Tyler had spotted the crocodile and was desperately trying to swim to shore. But that robe was weighing him down, making it hard for him to make progress. He was struggling just to keep his head above water, his face contorted with fear and strain.

Paige considered jumping into the river, but every cat instinct fought against it. Besides, she was no match for that water reptile.

Suddenly, she froze. It was as if something had reached into her brain and grabbed it. She locked eyes with Tyler and realized she was sensing his thoughts. He had reached out telepathically to her. She could feel a powerful connection between them.

Fear rushed through her, and she knew it wasn't her own. Slowly, that fear transformed into deep concentration. Tyler ignored the approaching crocodile behind him and kept staring at Paige.

Power of the Cat, Paige heard inside her head. It sounded like Tyler's deep voice.

Power of the Cat, unite with me. Send away this enemy.

It was bizarre. Tyler was somehow tapping into her power as a witch and then actively using it. She literally felt like a conduit of power, and that energy was pouring into Tyler.

Power of the Cat, unite with me. Send away this enemy.

Tyler's eyes never left hers, yet somehow he was using the magic on the crocodile behind him. Paige could see the creature stop and slowly turn around. Soon it was paddling down the Nile, far away from them. Tyler was safe.

Paige stumbled backward, as if a cord tying her to Tyler had been cut. She felt exhausted, the way she did after serious demon fighting. She flopped over and lay on the dock, panting.

That's a new one, she thought. *Tyler must have some innate power after all.*

Tyler pulled himself up onto the dock. He knelt in front of Paige, dripping wet. "Thank you for your help, Bastet," he said formally. Water streamed from his hair, leaving a puddle.

Paige's tail flicked. She felt guilty. She had dunked Tyler into the Nile, and now he was thanking her. Mostly, though, she was confused. What had Tyler done? What did it mean? With whom was she dealing?

And could it help her turn back into a human?

She tried sending him a message. *Tyler, I'm not a cat. I'm a woman named Paige.*

Tyler stood up. "These clothes weigh a ton when they're wet," he complained.

Oh, well. The communication must go only one way.

He stripped off the ceremonial robe, leaving only the pleated linen skirt.

Paige's tail flicked again. His dark skin contrasted sharply against the white linen. He was slim, with a swimmer's lean body. *He'll fit in a lot better with the rest of the Egyptian population now,* Paige realized. Most of the men went around in those little skirts.

Tyler hung the robe from a nearby branch. "In this heat it should dry quickly." He glanced up at the sky. "Though the sun will probably set soon.

"We should probably try to find some shelter before nightfall," Tyler continued. "It will get awfully cold once it gets dark."

Paige shuddered. *Not to mention all the creepy crawly desert creatures who may show up once it gets dark.*

"I suppose we could barter some more of your jewelry for a bed," Tyler mused. "But I'd rather hold on to that in case of emergency."

Isn't being stuck in 1200 B.C. an emergency? Paige wondered. But her jewelry wasn't going to get her home. She figured the kind of emergency Tyler had in mind was more in the food and water category.

Tyler paced along the dock. Paige trotted alongside him, being careful not to trip him again.

Tyler came to a sudden stop, nearly stomping on one of Paige's paws. He snapped his fingers. "I've got it!"

"What?" she demanded. "What have you got? Just because I'm a cat doesn't mean I don't deserve to know your plans. What affects you affects me, too, you know."

But, of course, he didn't answer her. He picked her up, grabbed his robe off the branch, and strode away from the Nile and back into the heart of the town. He found his way back to the very temple in which they had originally arrived.

"Uh, Tyler," Paige said in a tentative meow, "you having a short-term memory problem? We orbed out of here to avoid being impaled by a pack of guards with spears."

"Don't worry, little cat," Tyler crooned. "I know they scared you here. But you have nothing to worry about."

"Yeah, right," Paige replied. "I believe that."

Tyler knocked on the door. Paige braced herself for an attack.

A short, stout man with a shaved head opened the door. Paige judged him to be about fifty years old.

"Yes, foreigner?" the man asked.

"I would like to join your House of Life," Tyler said.

Huh? Paige craned her head around to look up at Tyler. What was he talking about? And why did he sound so sure of himself? *Oh, right,* she reminded herself, *this is Tyler. He's always sure of himself now that he's in Egypt.* In the short time she'd been with him, she'd certainly learned that lesson!

The man looked skeptical. "Why would we invite you in, foreigner?"

"I am Tyler . . . amses. Tyleramses. I was an apprentice to a master. I have many skills, and I have dedicated myself to Bastet. This is where I want to be and where I can offer my services."

"We have many talented scribes," the man said. "Why should we add another to our staff?"

"My skills are special. I know all the most secret powers of writing. I can harness the energy of the signs and symbols to do my bidding."

He was going too far. *He's going to get us arrested or killed. Or at the very least, he's going to blow our opportunity for a warm bed.*

"You make great claims, stranger. Can you prove what you say?"

"With the help of Bastet, yes, I can."

Paige felt his thoughts reaching for hers again: *Power of the Cat, unite with me. Bring me papyrus for this scribe to see.*

Paige felt herself tingle the way she did when she orbed objects. In a moment a papyrus roll, the paper that ancient Egyptians used to write on, shimmered and appeared in Tyler's outstretched hand.

The older man instantly bowed. "You may enter. We are honored to add such a talented magical scribe to our group."

"Thank you. I only want to learn."

Okay, Paige thought, *what's going on here?*

Tyler had tapped into her magical abilities again. *He obviously has some kind of dormant power,* she surmised. *Which means there has to be some way to work this so that we can understand each other.*

Paige reached out to Tyler with her mind, trying to probe for some link, some connection. "Tyler," she said, "it's me, Paige. Only you know me as Bastet, your cat."

She saw Tyler's eyes flick to her. But he didn't respond, he just followed the priest into the temple.

Even though Paige's experiment hadn't quite worked, she had noticed . . . something. She was determined to try again. *I am not giving up on this,* she vowed.

The House of Life, Paige discovered, wasn't an actual house, but a section of the temple devoted to students learning to become scribes. There were classrooms as well as sleeping chambers. The man brought Tyler and Paige to a very comfortable-looking room.

"This is for honored guests," the man explained.

Paige gazed around a beautiful room. There wasn't much furniture—just a long narrow bed piled high with cushions and a painted chest and two small tables—but the tile floor and the painted walls were astonishing. Oil lanterns sat on the floor, exotic flowers stood in vases on the tables, and ornate ceremonial daggers were displayed on one wall.

Their escort showed Tyler the jugs for water and the plate of fig cakes by the bedside, then left the room. A moment later a serving girl arrived with linens for the bed, towels, and several elegant robes, which she lay on the freshly made bed. She backed out of the room, her eyes never leaving Tyler. Paige couldn't tell if she was in awe of his so-called powers or if the girl just thought he was cute.

Tyler peeled off his damp tunic and put on one of the gauzy robes. He tied it shut, then stalked around the spacious, airy room.

"I'm going to rule this joint," Tyler said. "I am awesome!"

Rule this! Paige thought. She leaped onto the bed and ripped one of his new robes to shreds. "Just you wait," she warned. "I'm not ever going to use kitty litter."

She figured that if she proved to him that he couldn't control a cat, he couldn't expect to control the universe!

But Tyler didn't seem to notice. He sprawled on the luxurious bed, gazing up at the painted stars on the ceiling.

"Oh, Bastet, isn't this great?"

He reached over and took a bite out of one of the fig cakes that had been left for him. He held it out for Paige to take a bite, but she just stared at him. She didn't really like the direction in which this conversation was going.

He popped the rest of the little fig cake into

his mouth. "Did you ever feel as if you didn't fit in?" He looked at her and laughed. "How could you? Cats are so independent. They make themselves at home no matter where they are."

He leaned sideways and scooped Paige toward him, then sprawled again on his back on the bed. "For some reason, I've always been more attracted to ancient civilizations than my own. Any place seemed preferable to the place I was in. Being a scribe in the House of Life. Amazing! A lot better than that stupid mechanic's job I don't have anymore." He picked up another fig cake. "What's to go back to? Here I fit in. Here I could be happy.

"You'd be happy here too," he told Paige, stroking her dark fur. He rolled over onto his stomach and pulled Paige gently against him. "Cats are sacred here. You are as honored as I am. Probably even more."

He grinned happily. "Maybe I won't try to figure out how to reverse the spell. Maybe I'll just stay right here.

Forever."

Chapter
9

Piper drummed her fingers on the dining room table. For the tenth time, she popped up from her seat, gazed upward, and demanded, "What is taking so long?"

"He'll get here when he gets here," Cole said.

Piper crossed her arms. "That's helpful."

Phoebe lay a hand on Piper's shoulder. "All Cole is saying is that Leo will be back when he has all the information."

"I hope his sources are well informed," Piper said. "Because right now we have no hope of finding Paige on our own." She plopped back down in the chair. *Come on, Leo,* she thought.

As if he had heard her, Leo orbed in. Piper leaped up and grabbed her husband's arm. "Well? Did you find out where she is?"

Leo nodded. "You're not going to believe this."

Piper took a step backward and raised an eyebrow. "I don't like the sound of that."

"The Disciples of Thoth told you that the spell used responds to the intentions of the priest, right?"

"Right," Piper said cautiously, bracing herself for whatever shocker Leo was about to tell them. "And his intentions were . . . ?"

Leo took a deep breath. "Well, it seems that our cat lover Tyler wanted to go back in time." His blue eyes fell on Piper. She knew he was letting her know that she should prepare for this. She nodded for him to continue. "To ancient Egypt," he said.

"What?" Piper shrieked. All the warning in the world wouldn't have prepared Piper for that one.

"Cool," Phoebe exclaimed.

Piper shot her a look. "Excuse me?"

Phoebe shrugged and gave Piper a sheepish grin. "I've always wanted to check out an ancient civilization. Egypt is amazing."

"There was a lot of powerful magic there," Cole added. "Some of their inscriptions tell of extraordinary abilities."

"Hello?" Piper threw up her hands. "Am I the only one who finds this news more than a little freaky?"

"Sorry," Phoebe said. She gave Piper a hug. "Sweetie, we're all concerned about Paige. You shouldn't feel so much pressure just because you're the one who insisted on giving her away."

"Hey!" Piper smacked Phoebe's arm. "Did you have to remind me?"

"Here's some good news," Leo interrupted. Good thing, because Piper was getting irritated.

"Thank goodness. I could use some," said Piper.

"The gang upstairs was able to pinpoint the exact time and place Paige was taken to."

"Assuming she's still there," Cole warned. "If Tyler has this kind of power, who knows where they might be by now?"

Phoebe nodded. "We could be in trouble if Mesopotamia suddenly fascinated him."

"All the more reason to move quickly," Leo agreed. "We should be able to transport ourselves there by using the same spell, with the intention of traveling to the city of Bastetium, on the banks of the Nile, circa 1243 B.C."

"You mean you didn't locate the street address?" Piper teased. She felt hugely relieved. They'd find Paige after all and straighten out this whole thing. The Elders had interfered in their lives an awful lot, and Piper often resented it, but this time they really came through.

She turned to Phoebe. "Why don't you write a spell for added punch," she suggested. "We'll add that we want to be brought when and where she was taken."

Phoebe nodded. "Good idea. We don't want to spend time roaming the city."

"Cole," Leo said, "you should stay here. In

case she returns, or if the Elders have any other information."

"Got it."

"Are you coming with us?" Piper asked.

Leo nodded. "We're not sure if this spell is reversible. I want to be able to orb you all out of there if I have to."

"Yeah," Phoebe added. "We also don't know if Paige can orb as a cat."

Piper sank back into her seat. Time travel. Worrying about whether or not her sister could perform magic in a cat's body. Too weird. But just another day in the life of a Charmed One.

Phoebe sat down with a pen and paper. In a few minutes she looked up from the pad. "Got it."

Leo, Piper, and Phoebe huddled together. Phoebe held the paper out so that Piper could see it.

> *Separated by time,*
> *Separated by space,*
> *Reunite us three*
> *In our sister's current place.*

Piper looked at Phoebe. Phoebe shrugged. "So it's not my best work. I was in a hurry."

"Concentrate on where you want to be," Leo instructed. "I'll join in during Tyler's incantation."

Piper was glad Leo had decided to come along with them. She always felt safer with him beside her.

Piper focused her mind, first filling it with images of ancient Egypt that she remembered from school, from museums, and from educational programming on TV. She could sense that Phoebe was doing the same thing. She opened her eyes as she felt Phoebe move the slip of paper back into view.

They began the incantation, repeating it over and over, and this time Piper pictured Paige. Then she wondered if she should picture her as a cat, since that was the form she was in right now.

Leo's voice brought her back to the spell. Together they spoke the words they had heard in the temple:

> *Ancient wise ones,*
> *Link to my will*
> *My greatest desire*
> *Now you fulfill.*

Over and over again, their voices chanted. *Will it work?* Piper worried. *It must!*

Piper felt a strange whoosh—nothing like the orbing she was used to doing with Leo. She felt as if she were taking off on the fastest plane she'd ever ridden. Even though her eyes were closed, images hurtled past her. She gasped. She was watching the world going back in time— like a video in reverse. A roaring sound filled her ears.

Then silence.

Piper's eyes popped open. She was standing in a dark temple, its walls covered in colorful paintings. The place was cool, almost chilly. She glanced around. Enormous columns carved in intricate patterns loomed over her. The place was huge.

A life-size statue of a woman with a cat's head stood in front of them. Beyond it loomed an enormous cat sculpture.

Her eyes adjusted to the dark environment, and she realized an altar was set up in front of the cat-woman statue.

And on the altar was a little, dark kitty cat.

"There she is!" Piper cried. She dashed forward.

As she approached the altar she noticed the cat wore one serious necklace. "Now that's living large," Piper told the cat. She picked her up off the altar.

The cat resisted. "Paige, come on," Piper said. "I know you're mad at me, but don't you want to go home?"

Piper glanced around, wondering where Tyler was. "So where's your traveling companion?" she asked.

The cat stared at her.

"What's the matter, cat got your tongue?" Piper quipped.

She sighed. They probably shouldn't leave without Tyler. From the way the Disciples of Thoth had been talking, Tyler wasn't someone with a whole lot of magical experience. He might wind up stranded here by himself. "Okay," she told the cat, "we'll try to find him. And I'm hoping you've got some idea of where he is."

Piper walked down the little steps that led up to the altar. As soon as she hit the tiled floor, the cat let out a loud howl.

"Look, we can work this all out when we get home, okay?" Piper walked toward Leo and Phoebe. The cat yowled again, this time even louder.

Suddenly, two guards carrying spears emerged from the shadows. One of them pointed at Piper and shouted something incomprehensible.

"I might not understand the language," Piper told the cat, "but I definitely get the meaning."

Before she could move, a net dropped onto her from the ceiling. She was trapped.

"Piper!" Phoebe yelled.

"Orb us over to Leo!" Piper yelled at the cat. The cat just stared at her as if she were crazy.

Great. Paige can't orb in this form. Piper tried to freeze the guards coming toward her, but clutching the squirming creature made her aim go wonky. She missed the guards completely. She stopped two mosquitoes midflight instead.

"Just get over it!" she shouted at the cat. "Quit fighting me." She spat netting out of her mouth and called to Leo and Phoebe. "Paige isn't letting me freeze them!"

"On it!" Phoebe yelled. She and Leo raced toward Piper. Piper desperately tugged at the net, which wasn't easy with the hissing, spitting, scratching cat in her arms. Glancing up, she could see Phoebe take out a guard in a single roundhouse kick. As Phoebe launched herself at the other guard Leo raced past them and helped Piper get out from under the net.

"Now, Phoebe!" Leo shouted.

Phoebe sprinted over the fallen guard to where Leo and Piper stood waiting. They flung their arms around her.

"Stop scratching me," Piper hissed at the cat. The cat hissed back.

"Watch it," Piper snapped, "or we'll leave you like this and give you away again."

Piper felt Leo's orbing power whoosh them back to their own time. She instantly dropped the cat to the floor. It raced under the couch.

"You'd better hide," Piper warned. She examined her arm. It was covered in cat scratches.

"What is with her?" Piper complained. "Was what I said so terrible?"

"Maybe there's something in the shape-shifting spell that makes her different," Phoebe suggested.

"Honey, I'm so glad you're safe," Cole said, taking Phoebe into his arms.

"Me too. But most of all, I'm glad Paige is safe."

Piper snorted. "I'm not so sure about that at the moment."

"Let's do the reversal spell." Phoebe dropped down onto all fours and peered under the couch. "Come on, Paige. Time to turn back into yourself."

She sat back on her heels. "I don't think she wants to come out."

"I'm not going after her," Piper said. She held up her scratched arm. "I've already been wounded in the line of duty."

"Let me try." Leo knelt down and extended a hand. "Here, kitty, that's a good girl." He used a very soothing tone.

If that didn't get Paige out from under the furniture, Piper didn't know what would.

"That's right, I'm not going to hurt you."

Piper saw Paige's little cat head emerge from under the sofa. Whatever Leo was doing, it was working.

The cat crept out, never taking her eyes off Leo. "Good little cat," he crooned. He picked her up and cuddled her in the crook of his arm. "See? You just have to know how to talk to her."

Piper raised an eyebrow at Leo. "Well, usually that sisterhood, girl-power thing is good enough."

Leo shrugged. "Maybe her Whitelighter half is stronger in this form, so she responds more to me."

"Well, we can ask her all about it once she has a human mouth and can talk again," Phoebe said. "Let's get this taken care of now, before our little respite from demons is over."

"Good thinking."

They went up to the attic while Cole stayed downstairs on demon patrol. Piper found the entry for shape-shifting in Book of Shadows and flipped through it, searching for the reversal spell.

Hmm. There was one for the spell-caster to do herself to turn back. *Why hasn't Paige done that?* Piper wondered. She shook her head. Of course. Paige had probably been so eager to try the spell that she didn't even read the second and third pages.

"Hey," she said, "it says here that the ritual gives the witch the power of animal transformation. Once she does that, she can change into other animals too, until the magic wears off."

"Let's not wait for her batteries to run down," Phoebe said, joining Piper at the lectern. "Let's just take care of this now."

"Okeydokey."

There was another incantation to use to reverse the spell by someone else. *Must be a backup,* Piper surmised, *in case the witch had trouble doing it herself.*

> *Return to who you were*
> *Remember who you are*
> *No longer animal—*
> *Become human once more.*

Piper and Phoebe chanted while Leo held the cat still. After the third time there was a rustling breeze through the attic, which always signaled magical energy. In an instant the cat in Leo's arms transformed into a woman.

A very beautiful woman.

Only that woman wasn't Paige!

Chapter
10

Phoebe's jaw dropped. Their mistake was all too obvious. They'd grabbed the wrong cat!

"All clear downstairs," Cole announced, coming into the attic. "How is everything up here? Uh, what's going on?"

Everyone in the room stared at Leo and the gorgeous woman he held in his arms. She had dark skin, deep-set brown eyes, high cheekbones, and full, sensuous lips. She wore a white robe, a lot like the clothing they had seen at the Disciples of Thoth meeting.

There was something very feline about her, Phoebe noted. *Well, duh. She was a cat not too long ago.* Somehow they had turned a cat into a woman! Shape-shifting was definitely a complex art. For advanced witches only.

The woman gazed adoringly at Leo, who gazed back—not adoringly, but with confusion.

Piper was the first to speak. "Uh, Leo . . . maybe you should put the kitty down. Now that she's no longer a kitty?"

Phoebe suppressed a grin. She knew her sister well enough to know that tone. Piper was fighting back total annoyance. Not just because they had made a mistake. This irritation was fueled by just the teensiest bit of nonmagical jealousy. The former cat was a total knockout.

Leo blushed crimson up to his blond hairline. Hastily, he lowered the woman so that her bare feet touched the floor. "Sorry."

The woman said something to Leo that Phoebe didn't understand. Neither did Leo.

"Huh?" he said.

The woman repeated herself, still completely unintelligible, in that same mysterious language.

Phoebe and Piper exchanged a confused look.

"How's your ancient Egyptian?" Cole asked. "I think that's what she's speaking."

"What?" Phoebe stared at him.

"I ran into a few speakers back in my demon days," Cole explained.

"So what did she say?" Piper asked.

Cole shrugged. "I just recognized the language. That doesn't mean I can speak it."

The woman stood watching them, clearly as confused as they were.

"Why don't you whip up a translation spell?" Leo suggested.

Phoebe nodded. "Uh, let's see." She took

Piper's hand, then shut her eyes to help her concentrate.

> *"Visitor from another land,*
> *We need help to understand.*
> *Let our words now be clear*
> *When we speak, both far and near."*

"What happened to me?" the woman asked, her voice husky.

Almost like a purr, Phoebe realized.

"Where am I?"

"We kind of goofed," Phoebe explained, even though the woman had been talking to Leo. "We were actually trying to bring back our sister. Instead, we got you."

"Bring her back?" the woman asked.

"From your time. And your shape, as a matter of fact," Piper said. "She's a cat too. For the moment."

"We've brought you into the future," Leo explained. "Into our time."

The woman's eyes widened. "How exciting. You must be a very powerful sorcerer," she said to Leo.

"Actually, he didn't have a whole lot to do with it," Piper said. "But now we have to return you to where and when you came from."

"No!" The woman backed away. "I want to stay here."

"I bet you do, Kitty," Piper muttered.

"Conference," Phoebe announced, grabbing Piper's hand. She dragged her to the corner of

the attic. Piper's eyes kept flicking back to where
Kitty stood with Leo.

"Listen," Phoebe said. "I don't think we can
take her back right now. We can't waste time figuring out how to reverse the spell that just
turned the cat into a woman."

Piper crossed her arms over her chest. She
looked like she still needed convincing.

"We need to get Paige back here before something happens in ancient times that we can't
undo. What if Tyler decides to time travel again?
We can't risk it."

"Oh, okay," Piper agreed reluctantly.

They crossed back to where Kitty had curled
up on an old trunk beside Leo. Cole hovered in
the doorway.

"It's like this," Piper said. "You'll stay here
with Leo."

"Oh, good," the woman said, smiling.

"Don't get used to it," Piper warned. "The
minute we come back, it's back to ancient Egypt
with you. And back to fur balls."

Phoebe grabbed her sister's arm again and
dragged her back to the corner. Cole followed them.

"What?" Piper snapped.

"Keep it cool," Phoebe whispered to Piper. "We
don't want her running out on us. Who knows
what she would get up to out there on her own?"

"I'm more worried about what she's going to
try getting up to here," Piper hissed back.

"Leo can handle it. She seems to have taken a

liking to him," Phoebe admitted. "Must be the lion reference." Piper stared at her blankly. "You know. Leo. The lion. Get it?"

Piper glared at her through narrowed eyes. "Oh, I got it. I just didn't think it was funny."

"Sorry."

"I'll stay here and chaperone," Cole offered. Phoebe saw that Piper looked a little more relieved. Not a lot. But at least less like she was going to get into a cat fight with the former cat.

"Are you sure you don't need me to come with you?" Leo asked.

"I think we can manage on our own," Piper assured Leo. "Our magic worked fine. We can spell ourselves back here."

"We promise to call you if we get into any trouble," added Phoebe.

They repeated the spell they had used earlier. They found themselves back in the exact same spot as they had before.

Only this time the guards were ready for them.

"Seize them!" one of them yelled. Before either sister could move, the guards had grabbed them roughly by the arms, making it impossible for Phoebe to toss any energy balls or for Piper to do any freezing.

"I guess that translation spell works in ancient Egypt too," Piper commented.

So much for being able to take care of things, Phoebe thought.

Chapter

11

Paige's triangular cat ears stood straight up on her head. She couldn't believe what she was hearing. Stay here? No way! Paige leaped up onto Tyler's chest and meowed all of her protests into his face.

"What's wrong, Bastet?" he asked. "What has gotten into you?"

"What's gotten into me?" Paige shrieked. "What has gotten into *you*? What would make you think it would be okay to stay here?" She dug her claws into his shirt.

"I wish I could understand you," Tyler said in a soothing tone. "Then maybe I could do something to fix things."

"Yeah, bud?" Paige snapped. "The feeling is mutual." In a huff she disentangled her claws and paced along the bed.

"Wh-What did you say?" Tyler sat up and

114

grabbed her. He stared into your face. "Did you say something?"

"Hey, don't squeeze so hard," Paige complained in a whimpering mew.

"Sorry." Tyler released her. They each did a double take.

"Did you just . . . ?" Paige sputtered.

"This can't be possible," Tyler blurted. He grabbed her again and held her up so that they were eye to eye. "Say something," he ordered.

"Can you actually understand my meowing?" Paige asked slowly.

Tyler's almond eyes widened. Then he nodded. "Yes, Bastet. I can understand your language."

"Well, it's about time!" Paige swiped at Tyler, to get him to release her. She landed with a thud on the floor. "Okay, Tyler, we have some serious talking to do."

"You're right!" he said excitedly. "This means I truly am becoming more and more powerful. Now I can understand the language of animals. Is there no limit to my—"

Paige nipped his ankle. That shut him up. "Let me rephrase. *I* have a lot of talking to do. I've been listening to you all day. Now it's your turn to listen to me."

Tyler sat back down on the bed. "Okay," he said. Paige could tell he was a little bewildered by being ordered around by a small cat. Well, he'd just have to get over it.

"First of all, I'm not a cat. I'm a witch. And my name isn't Bastet. It's Paige."

He looked completely mystified. "Uh, pleased to meet you, Paige. But why—"

Paige held up a paw. "This will go a lot faster if you don't interrupt."

"Okay, okay. Just don't bite me again."

Paige paced back and forth in front of the bed. "I turned myself into a cat while I was practicing a shape-shifting spell, and before I could figure out how to turn myself back, my sisters brought me to the animal shelter."

"Where I found you," Tyler said.

"Exactly. The next thing I knew, you were whisking us back in time to a Cecil B. DeMille flick. And now we need to work together to get us back home. Pronto."

Tyler shifted nervously on the bed. "I—I don't think I know how to do that," he confessed. "I don't even know why the spell worked. I've tried dozens of them before, and this was the very first time anything happened."

"I think the reason it worked had to do with me," Paige explained.

Tyler looked perplexed. "What do you mean? It wasn't my power?"

"Hate to disappoint you, but, no. You said it yourself—nothing has ever worked before. Until you brought me into the mix."

"Oh," he said softly. "Did I at least get us out

of the temple when the guards burst in?" he asked hopefully.

"Sorry. That was me too. It's kind of what I do. It's called 'orbing.'"

Tyler looked so crushed that Paige actually felt sorry for him. He had been so pleased with himself, and now he felt like a big nothing.

She hopped up onto the bed beside him. "Listen, I think you did have something to do with it too. There's something about the . . . *connection* between us that is a kind of channel for magic. I believe you have some innate power, and working together, I bring it out in you." She explained about the strange way she could hear his thoughts at the Nile when he saved himself from the crocodile and how the same thing happened with the papyrus when they arrived at the House of Life. "And just now you wished you could understand me, and you do."

Tyler's face brightened. "You're right. I turned you into a talking cat. That's something, anyway."

She decided not to tell him that as a Charmed One, she had way more power than he did and that it was far more likely that her attempts to communicate had probably finally worked. She didn't want to totally crush the guy's ego.

"So maybe if we work together, we can get home," Paige said.

"I just don't know," Tyler said. "I don't know

if we would need the whole ritual to make it work. And I'd hate to end up somewhere else by mistake."

Paige lay down and rested her head on her paws. "You're right. We have to think about this carefully." She let out a soft mew. "Will I ever be human again?"

Tyler stroked her fur. "Can't you just turn yourself back?"

Now it was Paige's turn to be embarrassed. "I didn't look that far ahead in the spell. I was too excited to try shape-shifting. How can I possibly perform magic as a cat? Besides, most spells require the use of my hands and my voice."

"You're speaking now," Tyler pointed out.

Paige cocked her head to the side. "You're right, I am." Then she flopped back down. "But I wouldn't know what to say. Phoebe is the one who can write spells. Besides, most of the time when I perform magic, it's with my sisters. Their power helps me. This is the biggest thing I've ever done on my own. And I messed up. Again."

There was a sharp knock at the door, and before Tyler could answer, a servant stepped into the room, accompanied by a guard.

"Yes?" Tyler asked. "Am I needed some-where?"

"Your presence is required for questioning," the servant replied. "You have been accused of fraud."

"Oh, great," Paige blurted. "Just what we need."

She and Tyler both froze, waiting to see how the servant and guard would respond to a talking cat.

The guard stepped forward. "Now," he ordered.

Tyler and Paige exchanged a look. "They can't understand me," she said. "I'm not a talking cat after all. It's that connection again."

"May I bring my cat?" Tyler asked the guard. "As you can see, she is upset. She always senses conflict."

"Of course," the guard said. "We always respect the wishes of a cat."

"In that case, I wish you'd bathe more frequently," Paige told the guard, knowing he'd never understand her. She could see Tyler fight back a smirk.

"Let's get this cleared up," Tyler said. He gave the guard a charming smile. "I'm sure it's all just a misunderstanding."

They were escorted through the living quarters, and then they were led into the administrative rooms. Tyler carried Paige into a large chamber. Like all the others, the walls were highly decorated, and the columns had been carved to look like trees. At one end a man was seated on a high chair. A scribe knelt by his side, pen in hand, his tools on the low table next to him. Men in robes sat in a row along one wall. There was another scribe at the end of the row, obviously ready to take notes. Flames in the oil lamps flickered, sending a pungent smell into the air. It tickled Paige's whiskers.

"You are the stranger known as Tyleramses?" the man in the chair asked.

"Yes, I am."

"I am Kuthra, royal scribe. News of your"—Kuthra paused, as if he was searching for the right word—"your *tricks* have come my way."

Uh-oh. The disdainful spin the royal scribe put on the word "tricks" told Paige they were in trouble.

"I am honored to meet the royal scribe," Tyler said. "I am uncertain, however, why such reports would lead me to this tribunal."

Paige's tail flicked with worry. The word "tribunal" had a very serious ring to it. Luckily, Tyler's knowledge of ancient Egypt should help them navigate this tricky situation.

"We take our duties seriously," Kuthra explained. "We frown upon any actions that would compromise our reputation of integrity."

"I would never do such a thing," Tyler protested.

"Parlor tricks," Kuthra sneered. "Sleight of hand. These are all beneath the position of the scribe. And fraud as a means to enter these sanctified walls—that is a serious crime indeed."

"My magical abilities are no parlor tricks," Tyler fumed. "This magic is real. Just as yours is—if you have the skills."

"Great, Tyler," Paige hissed. "Rile him up, why don't you?"

"As you can see, my precious cat, representative of the goddess Bastet, finds your accusation insulting."

"And I find your manner insolent," the royal scribe bellowed. "You seem to place your own powers above mine."

"Don't get into a magic contest," Paige warned. "We don't know what we can and can't do, remember?"

But Tyler seemed to be off in a world of his own. He was so into this ancient Egypt thing, he was playing it all up to the hilt. As if he really were a scribe with magical abilities instead of an out-of-work mechanic with an obsession for Egypt.

"I will be happy to demonstrate my abilities," Tyler said. He placed Paige on the floor, then straightened back up again. "If you heard of my earlier demonstration, you know that I can make objects appear at my bidding."

"So that's what you're up to," Paige said. "I don't know if I can orb accurately as a cat."

That seemed to worry Tyler; this was not the time to experiment. He switched gears. "I can also see around corners," he said. He glanced down at Paige and winked.

Much better. "I'm ready when you are." She slunk along the wall, ready to sneak out of the room.

"Tell us what is in the room behind that wall," the royal scribe said. He pointed to the wall on his left.

Paige crept out of the room. Once she was
sure no one was watching, she tried orbing. It
worked. She scanned the room and quickly
orbed back out.

She dashed back into the tribunal. Tyler had
his eyes closed and was humming deep tones.
She pawed at his leg.

Tyler opened his eyes. "Oh, have I been
ignoring you?" he said. He picked up Paige and
held her close to his ear.

"Swimming pool. Three gorgeous women
skinny-dipping. Two chairs. Three palm trees,"
she reported to Tyler.

"Well?" Kuthra demanded. "Enough stalling."

"First I must thank the royal scribe for suggesting I look into that room, for it is a delight to
the eye," Tyler said. "But shouldn't you have
asked the permission of the three lovely ladies? I
hate to have intruded on their privacy."

"Wh-What?" Kuthra said.

"Perhaps you didn't realize the room was
occupied?" Tyler said.

"I did not know that, no," Kuthra replied.
"You are still stalling. What is in that room?"

"A pool. The palm trees add a touch of the
outside to the indoor room. Brilliant decorating
scheme. You could use a few more chairs," he
added. "I don't know who the three beauties are
who are bathing, but the next time you ask someone to look into that room, you should warn
them so that they have a chance to get dressed."

A gasp went around the room. "The foreigner is right! He does have the magic."

"Is he a sorcerer, or is he a scribe?" Kuthra demanded. "If he is a sorcerer intent on doing Bastet harm, he must be put to death."

"If you would lend me the stylus and papyrus, I can show you my handiwork. That will prove I am a scribe—and prove my loyalty."

The two scribes looked up at Kuthra, uncertain of what to do. Tyler strolled to the nearest one and took the pen and paper from him.

Paige watched nervously. This was a test she couldn't help him with.

In a minute Tyler held up a piece of papyrus, covered with hieroglyphics. "This is my favorite passage from the Book of the Dead," Tyler declared. He strode over to Kuthra and handed it to him. "As you know, the very writing itself is magical." He turned and faced the room. "As scribes, we have access to the symbols that hold power," he said. "I'm sure my own abilities are nothing beside those of this honored group."

"Way to be humble," Paige told Tyler. "I think I should be the one to arrest you for fraud."

Tyler bent down and scooped her up again. "Is that all?" he asked the group. "Because, as you can see, my cat would like to return to her room."

"That's all. For now." Kuthra glared at Tyler.

Paige knew the other scribes were impressed but that they had seriously angered the main man. That could come back to haunt them. Tyler's whole humble act could wind up backfiring.

A man in the shadows stepped forward.

"Vizier," Kuthra exclaimed, "I had no idea you were there."

"Vizier?" Paige repeated.

"A high-up government official," Tyler whispered.

"I am quite impressed with our new scribe," the vizier said. "I would like him included at all the royal meetings."

Another buzz went around the room. *This must be a big deal*, Paige realized. And one that wasn't making Kuthra any happier.

"It is done," Kuthra said. He gave a small bow. So did Tyler.

"Walk with me," the vizier said to Tyler.

"If you wish," Tyler replied.

"Timely exit," Paige said. "I think Kuthra's about ready to blow his stack."

The vizier led them to the room next door. "I was on my way to take my nightly swim. Care to join me?"

Tyler grinned. "I sure would!"

"After that description I bet you would," Paige commented dryly.

The vizier opened the door to the large chamber. Paige scanned the area. No nudies in sight. The women were now lounging around the tiled pool wrapped in towels.

Paige's eyes bugged when the vizier dropped

his loincloth and dove into the pool. *I guess the attitudes are a little different here,* she thought.

A blush deepened Tyler's dark complexion. "Well, what are you waiting for?" Paige teased. "I thought you wanted to go for a dip."

"I probably shouldn't go swimming," Tyler said to the vizier. "I just ate, you know. My mother always told me to wait at least a half hour after eating before going for a swim."

"If you prefer," the vizier said. "The pool is here for all high-ranking officials and their families."

"Another time," Tyler said. He hurried out of the chamber so fast, Paige had to trot to keep up.

"Slow down, shy boy," she called. "I may have four legs, but they're all a lot shorter than yours."

Tyler stopped and waited for Paige to catch up.

"I'm guessing you're not much into nude beaches, either," Paige said.

"Okay, so I'm a little shy," Tyler admitted. "And now that I know you're not actually a cat . . ."

"I promise to turn my back when you change your clothes," Paige promised. "But we have something a lot more important to talk about."

"Like what?"

"Like the fact that you totally dissed the royal scribe. He was seriously put out about your making points with the vizier."

"I don't know. Those positions are appointed for life," Tyler explained. "It's not as if I'd replace him."

"Maybe. But doesn't having friends in high-up places influence things too?"

"I don't think it's an issue," Tyler assured her. "I'll just work hard to get him to warm up to me."

They walked into their room. A skittering movement under the bed set Paige's fur on edge.

"Scorpion!" she cried.

"Not just one," Tyler murmured. Paige's eyes traveled up the wall to where Tyler was pointing. She spotted another of the deadly creatures in the small high window above the bed. Scanning the room, she noticed three more of the nasty things.

"Don't move," Tyler instructed her. "A scorpion sting can kill you in minutes."

Paige didn't have to be told twice. She froze in her spot.

But her mind was going a mile a minute. *Now what do we do?*

Chapter

12

"Don't panic," Tyler told Paige.

"Easy for you to say. You're a lot bigger than I am."

"Fight the cat instinct to pounce on moving prey," Tyler instructed.

"Don't worry," Paige assured him. "Attacking those things is very far from my mind. I'm a lot more worried about them attacking me."

"There were charms and spells to ward off scorpions," Tyler said. "I think I can remember one."

"But, Tyler, you're not really a magical scribe," Paige screeched. "That was just an act to keep us from getting killed."

"I have to try. You said that you thought I might have powers," Tyler reminded her.

"I was just trying to make you feel better," Paige said.

"Great. Blow my confidence, why don't you."

"Fine. Try. I'll help all I can."

Once again, Paige felt Tyler's thoughts entering her mind. *Power of the Cat, unite with me. Banish these scorpions to eternity.*

He made some strange signs with his fingers, as if he were writing symbols in the air. He kept repeating the chant, drawing power from Paige and drawing the invisible images over and over.

One by one, the scorpions crept toward the high window and crawled out. Very quickly, the room was a scorpion-free zone again.

Paige stared at Tyler. "What did you—"

He cut her off. "Wait." He climbed up onto the bed. He licked his finger and traced symbols around the window. Then he did the same thing along the floor and the doorframe.

"There. That should keep them out."

"What did you do?" Paige asked, once he let her finish the sentence.

"I remembered the hieroglyphics for protection and the one for scorpions. So I put them together to protect this room from scorpions."

"That was smart." Paige was impressed. And she now knew for a certainty that Tyler had some kind of magical abilities; otherwise, the protection spell wouldn't have worked. "Now can you make one to protect you from the royal scribe?" she said. "He may send something a lot harder to vanquish next time."

"I think you're wrong about him," Tyler said. "There's no reason to think Kuthra was responsible for the scorpions getting in here."

"I can think of several reasons," Paige argued. "The biggest one being wanting to protect his rank. Political enemies were always offing each other in the olden days. Didn't you ever read Shakespeare?"

"Paige, we don't have to blame Kuthra for the scorpion invasion," Tyler said. "Scorpions are so common in Egypt that there were actually scorpion charmers on every payroll. Why else would there be so many charms and amulets to protect against them?"

"Maybe . . . ," Paige said reluctantly. "But as long as we're trapped here, I want you to be very careful. I don't want to lose a single one of my nine lives."

"Hey, not so rough!" Piper complained. "We're going willingly."

Piper's wrists were sore from the guard's viselike grip. They were being marched somewhere at a very quick pace.

They had quite an escort. Not only were she and Phoebe each being led by a guard who had their wrists bound with scratchy rope, but there were several more guards in front of them, beside them, and behind them. All carrying spears.

"It's like we're public enemy number one," Phoebe whispered.

"We're not going to make a break for it,"

Piper promised the guard who held her ropes. "Do you think you can let up a little?"

The guard grunted. "We have never had unauthorized entrances into the temple before, but since yesterday we have had three. Twice by you. We take no chances."

Piper and Phoebe were herded down a long corridor lined with empty cells with heavy iron gates. The cell block was dark and airless. The only windows were tiny slits in the mud bricks up near the ceiling. A few oil lanterns flickered from the floor, creating strange dancing shadows and illuminating the sandy dust their feet kicked up.

Piper's nose wrinkled. Whatever oil they were burning in those lanterns was quite pungent in the close space.

The guards shoved Phoebe and Piper into the very last cell and slammed the iron gate shut. As the guards turned to go Piper called out. "Wait! Why are we under arrest?" she asked for about the hundredth time. "We didn't mean to trespass."

One guard—the large, burly one—stopped and faced her. He took a step back toward the cell. The rest hovered in the background. They seemed to be afraid; they kept their spears pointed at Piper and Phoebe, and they clustered close together.

The burly guard glared at her. "Trespassing is the least of your crimes."

"What do you mean?" Phoebe asked. "What do you think we've done?"

"We saw you," the guard snarled. "You stole the sacred temple cat."

"But—" Piper tried to protest, but the guard cut her off.

"To harm a cat is a terrible offense. Punishable by death."

Piper's eyes widened. They were in *that* much trouble? And for the heinous crime of *cat-napping*? He had to be kidding. *Okay, judging from that grim expression, this is not a guy into jokes.*

"We would never harm a cat," she said, clutching the iron bars.

"We *love* cats," Phoebe said.

"In fact," Piper continued, leaning an elbow on the bar and affecting a casual, chummy tone, "you're never going to believe this, but I swear it's true." She gave a little laugh. "We were in the temple because we were trying to find our *own* cat."

"Totally true!" Phoebe added. "We were just heartbroken when our cat disappeared, and someone told us they had seen her in the temple."

"She looks exactly like your cat. It was an honest mistake," Piper said.

"Honest," Phoebe echoed.

The guard wasn't buying it. His square jaw tightened with anger. "Do you think I am a fool? Don't add lying to your list of offenses! Look at you!"

Piper self-consciously smoothed her long hair. "Well, we've been busy, and I haven't had a chance to fix my makeup or brush my hair."

"The way you dress. The way you speak. And your magic!"

"Magic?" Piper winced. She was kind of hoping he hadn't noticed the way they had orbed in and out and back in again.

The guard gripped his spear so tightly, his dark knuckles whitened. "It can only mean one thing. You two are demons fighting against our great cat goddess Bastet."

"We're not demons!" Piper protested. "You have no idea how wrong you are!"

"We're the good guys!" Phoebe exclaimed.

"The royal priests will know what to do with the likes of you," the guard snarled. He spun around and clapped his hands. All the guards marched back down the corridor.

"Wait! Please! We still haven't found our cat!" Phoebe yelled after them.

"Give it up." Piper sank wearily onto the hard cot. She squirmed, trying to find a comfortable position. It wasn't easy. The bed consisted of only a wooden frame crisscrossed with leather straps. *Are all beds in ancient Egypt like this, or is this cot part of a prisoner's punishment?* At one end of the cot there was a hard wooden headrest. She leaned her elbow on it and rested her head in her hand.

"So what do we do?" Phoebe asked, sliding onto the floor and leaning against the cot.

"Paige is still here somewhere," Piper reasoned.

"We have to try to find her, and then we have to get out of here."

"That's not exactly a news flash," Phoebe said. "How do we do that before we're sentenced to death for hurting a cat?" She looked up at Piper. "Don't you think that's taking animal rights to an extreme?"

Piper had stopped listening, her attention elsewhere. "Look at all these pictures," she said. The entire cell was covered in paintings. "Do you think the prisoners did them to pass the time?"

Phoebe shrugged. "I wonder how much time there is between being arrested and being put to death. You did hear that put to death part, didn't you, Piper?"

"Yes, Phoebe, I heard it." Piper stood up and stretched. "I was just taking a little breather there, checking out the graffiti. Okay. Back to crisis mode."

Piper paced the cell. Everywhere she turned, she saw more images, more symbols, more pictures of wild-looking fantasy creatures. They were distracting. She turned to face Phoebe so that she wouldn't keep fixating on them. "We should be able to magic ourselves out of here. Once we do that, we'll start searching for Paige."

"Sounds like a plan!" Phoebe scrambled back up to her feet. "So . . . what do you think the best way to break out of here would be?"

"Too bad it's Paige who's missing," Piper mused. "She'd orb us out or orb in the key or something."

"I don't remember seeing the guard actually lock the door," Phoebe said.

"Maybe he was distracted by our horrible appearance! Oh, it can't be that easy!" Piper went to the gate and pushed against it with all her weight. It didn't budge. "Okay. So it isn't that easy."

"How about a spell?" Phoebe suggested.

"Be my guest," Piper replied, waving her sister toward the gate.

"Uh, let's see. Okay." Phoebe cleared her throat.

> *"Open the door, open the gate. This is a*
> *crisis. We really can't wait."*

"To the point," Piper commented.

Phoebe repeated the incantation, and Piper joined in. A little shiver of magic coursed through her body.

"Ow!" She shrieked and fell backward away from Phoebe. She felt as if she'd gotten an electric shock! Phoebe looked stunned too. A wisp of smoke rose from the doorway, and Piper smelled something that reminded her of the time they fried some wiring at home.

"It's as if the spell short-circuited," Phoebe said.

Piper stepped up close to the gate, taking care not to touch it. She peered up at the walls around and above it. They were also covered in colorful hieroglyphics. "You know, I have a funny feeling this isn't ordinary graffiti."

"What do you mean?"

Piper turned to face her sister. "I think these drawings are spells. I think we've been shut up inside a cell specifically designed to hold witches."

"That is so not good," Phoebe moaned.

"You can say that again." As Phoebe opened her mouth Piper held up her hand. "But do me a favor and don't."

Phoebe flopped onto the cot. "Ow!"

"Sorry," Piper said. "I should have warned you about the bed."

Phoebe rubbed her face. "I know there's a joke here about making your bed and having to lie in it, but I can't think of one."

"Thanks for restraining yourself," Piper said. "Because being trapped in an antimagic cell is no laughing matter."

Chapter

13

Phoebe was officially bored. She was tired of studying the hieroglyphics of weird-looking creatures that covered the cell. Some of them were in very awkward places, and her entire body felt kinked up from crawling around and trying to figure out what they might mean. And she was seriously sick of sweating. Her twelve-hour roll-on was working overtime for sure.

And I would be very happy to never see sand again in my entire life, she thought as she wiped grit from the palms of her hands. Sand was in her hair, her eyes, her mouth, and her clothes. It was going to be quite some time before she wanted to hit the beach again.

Phoebe straightened up with a groan. She glanced over at Piper who was perched on the uncomfortable bed. Her sister had been sitting like that—unmoving—for over an hour.

"Uh, Piper, you okay?" Phoebe asked.

"We've been gone for a while," Piper said, her eyes staring into space.

"I'm sure Paige is still okay," Phoebe assured her sister.

Piper blushed. "I was thinking about leaving Leo alone with Kitty for all this time."

"Oh, sweetie." Phoebe sat down beside Piper on the wooden cot. "You have absolutely nothing to worry about."

"Did you see her throwing herself at him?" Piper protested.

"She can throw all she wants, Leo isn't going to catch," Phoebe assured her. "And the minute we get home, we'll turn her back into her former kitty self."

"And not a minute too soon," Piper grumbled. "Since Leo seems to affect her like catnip."

Phoebe's forehead crinkled. "Something's weird here."

"Everything's weird here," Piper said.

"I mean, weird back there. At home."

"I know. I was just worrying about it, remember?"

"The spell." Phoebe stood and started pacing. "The spell wasn't to turn a cat into a human."

Piper looked at Phoebe a moment, her eyes narrowing as she recalled the words of the spell. "You're right. It was to return someone to their original form after a transformation. Probably to cover all the bases so the spell could be reversed no matter what they had turned themselves into."

Phoebe nodded. "Exactly. So that means Kitty started out human too."

"So we didn't actually turn a cat into a person," Piper said, working it out.

"What we saw was a woman who had been a cat, turning back into herself."

Piper snorted. "I wonder if some ancient Egyptian irresponsible younger sister type accidentally turned herself into a cat too."

Phoebe laughed. "Hard to imagine a lot of that going around."

A crash in the hall startled her. Phoebe peered out the bars of her cell.

A young woman—no more than a teenager—stood in the corridor surrounded by broken shards of pottery. The jug she dropped must have held water, because there was a growing puddle on the floor. She stared at Phoebe with wild dark eyes.

"Are you all right?" Phoebe asked the girl.

"Did you say you witnessed a cat turning back into a woman?" the girl asked, her voice shaking. "A cat from our temple?"

"Yes," Phoebe replied. "Why? Do you know something about that cat?"

The woman looked stricken.

"What is it?" Piper asked, jumping up from the cot. "Why is this news so upsetting?"

"We must tell the priestess Tipket at once!" the girl said.

"But why?" Phoebe asked.

"Please," Piper begged. "We left her alone

with my husband. If there's something dangerous about her, we need to know."

The girl stepped carefully around the pottery
and approached Piper and Phoebe. "I shouldn't
even be talking to you. You're prisoners."

"We may be able to help," Phoebe told her.
"Who is Tipket?"

"Tipket is the high priestess in the temple of
Bastet, the cat goddess. Our community is dedicated to her."

"No wonder there are such strict laws about
the treatment of cats in this town," Piper said.

"That woman—the one who had been a cat—
her name is Hoptith. She is terribly evil. Tipket
turned her into a cat to protect our town and the
very gods themselves."

"Oh, this does not make me feel good." Piper
sat back down on the bed. She hugged her knees
to her chest and lay her head on her arms.

But her sister wasn't the woman who had
Phoebe's attention. The beautiful woman Phoebe
had last seen in their attic was now standing in
the corridor behind the young serving girl, smiling slyly. To make it so much worse, she wasn't
alone.

She had a slimy green demon with her.

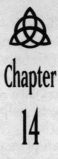

Chapter

14

"Piper," Phoebe hissed. "Get up, now."

"What?" Piper moaned, as she flopped over on the cot. "Can't I have just one minute for a minor freak-out?"

"No, because we have a major problem right here in front of us."

Piper's head snapped up. She stared at the woman formerly known as a cat. She leaped off the cot.

"What have you done with Leo?" Piper screamed at the woman. How could she have left her husband alone with this sorceress? "If anything has happened to him, I'll—"

The woman laughed a deep, throaty laugh. "You'll what? Put a spell on me? I don't think so."

The serving girl backed up against the mud wall, trembling with fear. Piper gave her head a sharp shake, indicating the girl should go and get reinforcements, like this Tipket person. But the girl was too frightened. She sank to the floor, covering her face with her hands, whimpering.

Hoptith and the demon ignored her, staying focused on Piper and Phoebe.

Hoptith crossed to the cell and stood a few feet from Piper. "Don't worry. I didn't do any permanent damage to your consort."

"Husband," Piper corrected. Not that his marital status would make this woman back off.

Hoptith stroked her long black braid. "Your Leo is quite appealing. It would have been a shame to harm him. I just . . . kept him out of the way." She tossed her braid over her shoulder. "I think when I return to your time, I'll keep him. Certainly he'll prefer me to you."

"I wouldn't bet on that," Piper spat out.

The woman chuckled. "I am irresistible; he'll thank me."

She snapped her fingers, and an ornate mirror studded with glittering gems appeared in her hand. She smiled at herself in the mirror. "Yes. As I remembered. And my powers aren't rusty after all that time." She brought down the mirror sharply, and it vanished again.

"I was right to join with you, Hoptith," the demon said. He stepped closer to the cell. Instinctively, Piper backed up. His foul stench wrinkled her nose. "You have done well."

Hoptith's gaze flicked from Piper to Phoebe. "So these are those you call the Charmed Ones, Kraken. Funny, they look so ordinary."

"Don't let appearances fool you," Piper snarled. "We pack a wicked wallop."

"I thought you said there were three," Hoptith said to Kraken.

"There are," Kraken said. "But two is enough for my purposes."

"And therefore mine." She faced the demon. "You will remember your promise."

"Certainly. You deliver the Charmed Ones, and I transfer new powers to you."

Piper smirked. "What powers could you possibly transfer to her?" She recalled the details Cole had given them about this brand of demon. "He doesn't have any powers of his own," she told Hoptith.

"That's right!" Phoebe seconded. "He just hangs around stronger beings trying to soak up random magic."

Piper caught the tiniest flicker of doubt flash in Hoptith's yellow-flecked eyes. Their words were having an effect.

If we can drive a wedge between Hoptith and this demon, we might have a fighting chance, Piper thought.

She sneered. "I don't know where you're getting your information, but this guy and his buddies are all low-level, bottom-feeding types."

"Don't listen to them," the demon snarled.

"Struck a nerve, fish face?" Phoebe taunted.

"Silence!" Hoptith commanded. She pointed her pinkie finger at Kraken. Sparks crackled as she raised him off the floor.

At least this spurned the serving girl into action, Piper noted. The girl crawled away as fast as her hands and knees could move.

The demon dangled in the air.

"What powers can you offer me?" Hoptith demanded.

"Please, put me down," Kraken begged, his voice choked. He looked as if whatever was holding him in the air were gripping him around the throat.

"I ask you—do these witches speak the truth?"

The demon clutched at his flapping gills. "I may not have prestige and rank, but I assure you, I have powers. Stolen, yes. But mine to give."

Hoptith lowered him back to the ground. She wasn't gentle about it. He landed with a thud and sprawled on his back, trying to catch his breath.

Hoptith stood over him, glaring. "If I find you have lied, you and all your spawn will regret it. Do you understand?"

"Yes," Kraken muttered.

"Yes, what?" Hoptith kicked him.

"Yes, most honored and revered, she whose powers darken the sun, Hoptith, queen of chaos."

"Whoa. That is one fancy moniker," Piper commented.

"Think she can fit that title on a business card?" Phoebe murmured.

Hoptith allowed Kraken to get back to his feet, but she still seemed annoyed. "I am concerned that your low rank will diminish my exalted position," she fretted.

"But, Queen of Chaos," Kraken protested, "once I destroy the Charmed Ones, I shall be considered lord of all the underworld."

"Hmm." Hoptith tilted her head to one side, studying him.

"Besides, I am the only one who can bring you to that new world. Where no one will turn you into a cat."

Hoptith nodded. "You do have a use, then. And what a world," she purred. "So much to conquer. So much power to tap into."

Interesting. Hoptith can't time travel on her own. Piper filed that information for future reference.

Hoptith smiled with satisfaction and returned her attention to Piper and Phoebe. "I suppose I should thank you," she told them. "For restoring me to my natural form."

She smiled, her gold-speckled eyes glittering. "I really am spectacular, aren't I?" She twirled in front of the cell. She was obviously enjoying being human again.

Piper recoiled from the woman. She could

feel the evil radiating from her. Why hadn't she sensed it before?

"If you're so grateful, why don't you dump the demon and work with us," Piper suggested, still trying to appeal to Hoptith's lust for power and rank.

"Oh, that wouldn't do at all," Hoptith said. "I need to get back to work. Good witches would just interfere."

"What work is that?" Now Piper was just stalling, trying to buy some time to figure out how to battle her and Kraken. She hoped Phoebe's brain was working better than hers.

"That silly Tipket, the high priestess, got in my way. I should see about doing something about her while I'm here."

"How did she get in your way?" Phoebe asked.

"I was working with high-level demons," Hoptith said proudly. "Practicing the dark arts. Tipket stumbled into one of my rituals. My goal was to take down the gods of order and begin my reign of chaos. And I would have won—if I hadn't been interrupted. Now I can set all that right."

"Your plan will succeed," Kraken assured her.

Way to kiss up, Piper thought.

"I do sense power from these two," Hoptith said. "They are strong."

"They've taken out many demons," Kraken warned.

"Then we shall take care of them from a distance," Hoptith said.

"What do you have in mind?" the demon asked.

"We'll use the incantations as they were meant to be used. You see these drawings?" Hoptith waved at the pictures covering the cell walls.

"Yes." Kraken hung on her every word. So did Piper, but for very different reasons.

"Used in conjunction with the right ritual, I can unleash the power contained in these symbols," Hoptith explained.

The demon rubbed his webbed hands together. "Now that I'd like to see."

"Don't encourage her," Piper snapped at the demon. She knew it! She knew those hieroglyphics were more than decorative.

"*Ho Tyranto Klepanth, Welisk calorinto set,*" Hoptith chanted.

Piper clutched Phoebe's arm. The walls of the cell seemed to be wavering. "Wh-What's happening?" she stammered.

"I think this cell is about to become very overcrowded," Phoebe replied.

Piper couldn't believe it. She stared at the drawing in front of her: The strange creature had the body of a man but the head of a wolf. As she watched, the picture writhed and shifted. It grew larger and larger, and as it expanded it became three-dimensional. It leaped off the wall, its fangs bared. Drool dripped from its sharp teeth, and the cell was filled with a foul animal stench.

The drawings on the wall were coming to life!

Chapter

15

"Man, you should do something about that breath," Piper told the wolfman. She shot out her hands and instantly shattered the creature. Now that she had the skill to speed up molecules so quickly that they exploded, she could take out monsters and not even have to clean up after them.

"On your left!" Phoebe shouted. Piper swerved out of the path of a glowing energy ball. It zipped past her but ricocheted off the cell gates, bouncing wildly around the cramped space.

"Yikes!" Piper dropped to the floor, covering her head.

"The inscriptions!" Phoebe cried. "They deflect the energy balls."

"Then quit throwing them!" Piper ordered from the floor.

"Then what should I—?" Phoebe cut herself off. "Above you!"

Piper rolled over and glanced up just in time to see a snake slither off the ceiling toward her. It was too close to shatter—she didn't want to impale herself on flying snake shards—so she froze it. It hung midair, just above her head.

The cell was a mass of swirling creatures. The pictures shimmered and grew, and as they came to life a deafening cacophony of animal howls and cries added to Piper's horror.

Phoebe slammed a monster with two squashed pig heads into the wall. On contact, it burst into flame, then sputtered out.

"I've never seen a demon do that before," Phoebe shouted over the wails and shrieks.

"They're not ordinary demons," Piper yelled back.

Piper blew her hair out of her eyes, not daring to use her hands for anything other than battle. A falcon with the face of a deranged woman flapped its wings in her face, and she saw that its talons were razor sharp. She flung up a hand, sending it flying across the room, but it recovered and swooped toward her again. She ducked down, twisted, and this time managed to shatter it.

She whirled around to see a miniature alligator knock Phoebe over with its thrashing tail. The minute Phoebe was down, a vicious monkey with completely transparent eyes leaped onto her. Phoebe let out a scream, and Piper crawled to her, afraid that her aim would go wrong in the cramped room and that any energy she sent out would ricochet, like the energy ball did, and hurt Phoebe. Piper tackled the monkey, and Phoebe kicked the alligator square in the snout. It reared up onto its tail and came crashing down again, just missing Phoebe as she rolled out of the way.

"There's no space to fight!" Piper panted. She kept having to freeze creatures instead of explode them, one after another. And whatever magic was used to create these relentless monsters, it messed with her power. The things would stay frozen only temporarily. But when she tried to explode them, they seriously blew up—bursting into flames. Dangerous in the tiny space.

Phoebe was fighting the old-fashioned way—with kicks, bites, and blows wherever she could land them. It seemed to confuse the creatures, as if they were used to magical battles and not fights with flesh-and-blood opponents. Piper wished she'd taken the martial arts classes Phoebe had—those skills would come in handy in this cramped fight.

A squat, winged hippo appeared, and Piper backed up against the cell door. "Yow!" she shrieked, feeling a shock jolt her as if she'd hit an electrified fence. Just as the protective incantations had intended.

She heard chanting behind her. Her heart sank. *Oh no. Has Hoptith come back? What is she going to do to us now?*

The hippo unfroze and charged toward her again, pushing her against the gate. But she didn't get shocked this time. Instead, the cell door popped open, and Piper tumbled backward onto the floor of the corridor.

"Don't stop fighting them," she heard a woman say behind her. "It will take a few minutes to return them to their written form."

"Got it," Piper responded. She didn't know what the woman had done to help them escape the cell, but she was grateful. "Phoebe! Make for the door! We can get out!"

Phoebe rolled out of the reach of another vicious monkey, and this time Piper slammed the creature with an energy ball. Direct hit. Phoebe raced out of the cell.

"Try to keep them in the cell," the woman commanded. Piper could see in her peripheral vision that the serving girl had returned, and she'd brought someone with her. A tall, strong-looking middle-aged woman stood in the hallway, making hand gestures and chanting in a commanding voice.

"We'll do our best!" Phoebe promised. She and Piper worked together to beat back the monsters that were trying to escape from the cell. Piper froze some and shattered others, while Phoebe launched energy ball after energy ball. *She's practically an energy ball assembly line,* Piper observed. One by one, the creatures shimmered, shrank, and returned to the cell walls.

For a moment the only sound was the raspy panting of the two Halliwells. After the deafening animal cries the quiet pounded hard in Piper's ears. Gradually, her breathing returned to normal.

"Thank you," she told the woman. "Who are you?"

"I am Tipket, high priestess for Bastet." She put a protective arm around the serving girl. "Mailin told me your story. If Hoptith is free, that is dangerous indeed for all of us."

"We didn't mean to undo your magic," Piper apologized. "We were trying to undo our sister's magic."

"I believe you are not in league with demons," Tipket assured her. "The spell on Hoptith was bound so that it could be undone only by good magic. I wanted to be sure no evil could free her, but I also wanted to allow for the possibility that she could change her ways. Obviously, she has not. We must find Hoptith before it is too late."

"I think she went back to our world," Piper explained. "Another country and another time entirely."

"She would want new worlds to conquer. She is as dangerous there as she is here. But here I can control her, if I can find her and do the spell again."

"We'd love to help you, but we have to find our sister first," Phoebe said. "We can't go back without her."

"Yes, your sister." Tipket seemed perplexed. "Mailin said the error occurred because you mistook Hoptith for your sister. Your sister is a cat?"

Piper understood the woman's confusion. The whole thing was one big weird misunderstanding. "She turned herself into one," she explained, "and probably can't turn herself back. She didn't mean to come here. A young man brought her from our time."

"We think that was an accident too," Phoebe added. "Has anyone new shown up at the temple? We're pretty sure this was where they arrived."

Mailin touched Tipket's bangled arm. "There is a stranger with magical abilities in the House of Life," she said. "He is said to have a cat with him."

"Is he good looking? With a short, trim beard?" Phoebe asked.

Mailin ducked her head to cover her embarrassment. "Some of the women may have mentioned his handsome face and nice physique."

"Sounds like our Tyler. Where is he?"

"He is staying in quarters for noblemen in the House of Life. It's part of the temple complex."

"Can you bring us there?" Piper asked. Finally, they were getting closer to tracking down Paige and possibly ending this fiasco.

"Yes, but we must take care," Tipket warned. "If we are caught . . ."

"What?"

"Helping prisoners escape is also a crime punishable by death."

Piper nodded, wanting the woman to know that she understood their risk. "Then we won't let you get caught."

Tyler lay propped up on billowy pillows, a dish of olives beside him. A pretty serving girl had just left. She had given him a massage with scented oils, peeled his grapes, fanned his face, and practically chewed his food for him. *She probably would have done that, too, if he'd asked!* Paige thought.

Paige's tail flicked. "Okay, buddy. Enough already. When are you going to get on the case?"

Tyler lifted a cobalt blue goblet to his lips and took a sip of wine. "What case?"

"The figuring out how to get us home case. Remember? We don't actually live here, you know."

"I know . . . ," Tyler said.

"You are enjoying all this far too much," Paige complained.

"I like it here. Is that a crime?"

"Well, I don't like it here. I don't like being a cat. And I don't like you taking all the credit for the magic!"

"Hey, I've got powers too," Tyler snapped. He scanned the room, then pointed to the water jug sitting in the corner. "Jug, fill yourself."

The jug trembled slightly. Tyler went to it and picked it up. It was obviously heavier now. "See?" He smirked at Paige. "Just a minute ago this was nearly empty. Now it's nearly full."

"You mean, now it's overly full," Paige said, watching water stream out of the narrow spout.

Tyler held the jug away from his body, trying not to get splashed. The water was coming faster now.

Tyler's smug expression became annoyed as water soaked the hem of his linen tunic. "Water, stop!" Tyler ordered. "Jug, empty."

"Need some help?" Paige offered.

"I can do this," he muttered. "Uh, water no more?"

Paige leaped onto the bed, wanting to keep her paws dry. "I guess you don't know your own magical strength," she said sarcastically. "That jug thinks you wanted a Nile-size water supply." She licked her front paw and casually began washing her face.

"Jug, stop! Don't do this anymore." Tyler paced around the room. He skidded on the wet tile floor, caught his foot in his dripping tunic, and fell. As soon as the jug hit the hard tiles, it smashed, and the water vanished.

Paige looked up from her cat bath. "I suppose that's one way to reverse the spell."

Tyler got up slowly and wrung out the hem of his wet linen robe.

"So, big shot," Paige taunted, "is amateur hour over?"

Tyler rubbed his face with his hands. Then he glared at Paige. "I wish I didn't understand you anymore."

Paige glared back, wondering if this wish had worked. "Well? Can you understand me?"

Tyler flopped back down on the cushions. "All too well."

Paige jumped up onto Tyler's chest. "Look, I can see that all this royal treatment can go to a guy's head. But enough already."

"Did you ever wonder why I spent so much time talking to you before I knew you were actually human?"

"Don't change the subject."

"This is the subject." Tyler's face grew serious. "All my life I've had trouble making friends. I felt more comfortable buried in a pile of books, pretending I lived in ancient times."

Paige cocked her head. "I find that hard to believe. I mean, look at you."

"What do you mean?"

"You're smart. You're a total hottie. And I think I've actually even witnessed you being charming."

He seemed genuinely surprised. "You think so?"

"Definitely. So what's with the loser label you've given yourself?"

Tyler shrugged. "I never seemed to be able to fit in. As a kid, I wasn't good at sports and was too . . . weird for the brains. And . . . I was bounced around from foster home to foster home after my mom died. It was hard for me to believe I'd actually know anyone long enough to forge a real bond. I've always felt more at home in my imagination—or in a museum."

"We all have places we retreat to," Paige assured him. "And you're not an awkward teen anymore." She knew from her work in social services what that sort of experience can do to a kid. But it didn't explain everything.

"This goes deeper than that," Tyler said. He sat on the bed beside her. "Much deeper."

Paige had the sense that Tyler was trying to rev himself up for some kind of revelation. "How so?"

"I just always connected to ancient Egypt. It's why I joined Disciples of Thoth. I wondered if maybe I had a real connection." He took a deep breath. "A magical one."

"That would explain a lot of what's been happening here," Paige conceded. "But do you have any real reason to think that?"

"My father vanished when I was little. And there were just things my mom said before she died—well, I got the feeling that he was not like other dads. And that maybe he disappeared because he didn't belong here." He grinned. "I mean, there. In the future."

"You mean, in our present," Paige corrected.

Tyler stood and waved at the pictures on the walls. "Look at this. These people. Do they remind you of anything?"

"My Ancient Civ exam?"

"Really. Take a close look at these figures."

Paige could tell Tyler was serious. She hopped off the bed, padded over to the wall, and stretched up. She placed a paw on the wall to steady herself.

The wall painting showed artisans working at their crafts. One was a scribe, another was a metal-worker, another a tailor. While the painting was beautifully detailed, the people themselves looked pretty much alike.

And exactly like Tyler—minus his beard.

"Are you . . . do you think you are a direct descendant of the ancient Egyptians?" Paige asked.

"Makes sense. As much as anything else. Maybe that's why I have some power. Not as much as you, of course." He gave Paige a wink. "But some. Maybe my father was a time traveler too. And that's why he couldn't stick around. And why all of this feels so right to me."

This line of thinking worried Paige. She sympathized; she certainly understood feeling disconnected and alienated. She also knew full well the powerful tug of family ties—particularly if you felt you were only just discovering them.

If the spell to return home depended on the wishes of the priest, she might never manage to get home at all. From the way Tyler was talking, he would never willingly return. How could she convince him to want to go? Somehow she didn't think offering to go on a date with him could compare to a world that fascinated him.

"I don't know what to say," Paige admitted. "I just know that we can't stay here. As much as you think you belong here, you're just a visitor." She jumped back up onto the bed, her tail flicking nervously. "Besides, you know how it is. Everything seems great on vacation. But once you settle in, you'd have to contend with things like scorpions and that pudgy Kuthra, who hates you, and—"

"Paige, it's okay." He lay a hand on her furry back, stroking it to calm her. "As much as I love it here, I know I don't have the right to keep you here with me. The only thing is, all I've been able to do so far is make spells, not unmake them. I don't know if I can get us home or not. But I promise I'll try."

Paige licked his nose. "That's all I can ask. And the minute we get back, we'll get you a real cat. One who is all feline, inside and out."

There was a soft knock at the door. "More treats?" Paige asked.

Tyler crossed and opened the door.

"My sisters!" Paige exclaimed. She dashed to the door and jumped up into Phoebe's arms.

"I'd say we found her!" Phoebe grinned.

"Phoebe! Piper!" Paige was so thrilled, she

could barely stay still. She wriggled up against Phoebe, and tapped Piper with a paw.

"So you're Phoebe," Tyler said. "And you're Piper."

"How did you know?" Piper asked.

"Paige just told me."

"You can understand her?" Phoebe asked.

"Looks like it. Just between us, I sometimes wish that I couldn't."

Paige swiped at Tyler's arm with her paw but kept her claws retracted. She knew he was joking.

"I know what you mean," Piper said dryly.

"Hey!" Paige stared at Piper. Was that a joke or not? No matter. She was so relieved that they had found her that she would let that cutting remark slide. For now.

"You are the new scribe," a tall woman said, stepping into the room.

This lady had no self-esteem issues, Paige observed. Strong, confident, and imposing. Paige admired her commanding presence. She seemed like a queen.

Tyler gave a slight bow. "I am. And I see by your robe that you are high priestess."

"Tipket," the woman introduced herself. "This is Mailin, my acolyte. I am teaching her the ways of the temple."

Mailin looked nervous. She kept glancing up and down the corridor.

"Come inside." Tyler waved at Mailin to

enter. She did quickly and shut the door behind her. "I think we have much to discuss."

"Can you turn me back into a human?" Paige asked her sisters eagerly.

"She sure talks a lot for a cat," Piper commented.

"She just asked you if you can turn her back into herself," Tyler translated.

"Oh, we definitely know how to do that spell. All too well." Phoebe explained about how they had accidentally used the spell on Hoptith.

"And now Hoptith is palling around with the dregs of the demon underworld," Piper said.

Phoebe bounced Paige in her arms. "The faster we get Paige human, the quicker we can kick some demon butt."

"I'm all for that!" Paige exclaimed.

Phoebe laughed. "I think I can guess what she said this time."

Phoebe put Paige on the floor, between her and Piper. She was so ready to be human again. Paige shut her eyes as her sisters chanted the reversal spell.

Did it work? Paige opened her eyes. She no longer had a cat's-eye view of the world from about twelve inches off the floor. She was now looking right into Tyler's handsome face.

Tyler's almond eyes widened with obvious attraction. "Wow."

"Back atcha," Paige quipped.

"If I had known you were this beautiful, I might have tried harder to reverse the spell," Tyler teased.

"Ah, it never would have worked anyway. You would have turned me into something else entirely by accident."

"Probably so," Tyler admitted with a sheepish grin.

Paige ran her hands up and down her arms, reveling in her human form. "It worked! I'm me again. Only two legs! No fur!" She flung her arms around her sisters. "Thank you, thank you, thank you."

Piper tugged Paige's arm away from her neck. "We have a few things to get straight," she scolded.

"I know, I know." Paige hung her head, then snapped back up. "Hey! You gave me away! Your own sister." She figured the best defense was a strong offense.

"I didn't know it was you!" Piper protested.

"You said I was barely housebroken!" Now that Paige remembered, she was mad all over again. If she had still been a cat, she would have hissed at Piper.

"Uh, let's not do this right now," Phoebe said.

"Yeah, let's wait until we're back home," Paige agreed.

"And when there isn't a demon standing behind you," Phoebe added.

Paige whirled around. And gazed up into a skull-like face towering above her.

And then another.

And another.

The room was filling up with demons!

Chapter

16

"Did you think Hoptith wouldn't notice that you escaped?" the largest skull-headed demon croaked. Paige's stomach curdled as she watched his superlong forked blue tongue dart around as he spoke. The creatures seemed to have no skin, as if they were walking skeletons.

"She is not pleased," another said.

"Hate to ruin the lady's plans," Piper said, "but she should be used to that. Being the queen of chaos and all."

"I thought her demon escort said there were two witches," another demon said. Paige thought he sounded nervous.

"Don't you know you shouldn't believe rumors?" Phoebe said.

Paige knew what she and her sisters could do, but she had no idea how Tipket, Mailin, and Tyler would handle themselves in a full-out demon assault. But there was no time to think about it.

"Dagger!" Paige orbed the weapon into her hands and plunged it into the demon on her right. He shattered into pieces. *Good.* She hadn't been sure if a dagger could damage something that had no flesh.

She ducked out of the way of a demon hurtling toward her, its blue tongue flicking in and out. She spun around and landed a solid kick in his midsection. He stumbled backward, directly into the path of one of Phoebe's energy balls. "Score!" she cheered.

Man, it feels good to have the use of my limbs again, Paige thought.

She was stunned to see that Tyler had created an energy ball. He flung it toward the demon nearest him, but it missed its mark and sent a jug crashing to the floor.

"Piper!" she cried, getting her sister's attention. She nodded toward Tyler, trapped in a corner. Piper froze the creature, then slammed the demon she'd been fighting into the wall.

"Agh!" A demon tackled Paige, and she fell to the floor, the wind knocked out of her. She kicked hard, feeling her feet making contact with bone, over and over. She managed to flip herself back over and faced the demon skull head-on. Struggling with all of her strength, she gripped the clawlike hands that held her around the neck, desperately trying to keep them from choking her.

She could hear Tipket and Mailin chanting strange words. The skeletal demon she battled shimmered and shrank. Her mouth dropped open in shock as it flattened out and pasted itself to the floor of Tyler's room.

Dazed, she got back up to her feet. *Oh no. Phoebe!* "Lantern!" Paige ordered. She made a sharp gesture, and the lamp smashed the demon who held Phoebe in a hammerlock. It broke his hold on her, and a few seconds later it, too, went from three dimensions to two, transformed by Tipket's incantation.

Paige heard Tyler shout behind her. One of the demons had whipped its blue tongue around him. Its two rows of teeth dripped with blood.

"It bit Tyler!" Paige screamed. She lobbed an energy ball at the demon. On contact, the creature sizzled and vanished, leaving only a foul smell in the air. Tyler collapsed onto the tiled floor.

"Help me!" Paige cried. "He's hurt!" She bent over Tyler, clutching his hand. His fingers were freezing cold, but his face was covered with sweat, as if he was burning up.

She craned her neck and saw Phoebe take out the last of the demons. "Please," Paige begged.

In a flash Piper knelt at her side.

"You'll be fine," Paige told Tyler as Piper examined his wounds. She hoped he believed her more than she believed herself. His dark skin was ashen. He looked awful.

"You did great," she told him, her voice shaking with concern and fear. "You held your own with a pack of demons,"

"Th-Thanks," Tyler said. His breath was shallow, and Paige could tell it was a struggle for him to speak.

"He's been poisoned," Piper told Paige quietly. "He's also lost a lot of blood."

Paige's heart clutched as Tyler's grip loosened, then his hand fell out of hers. His eyes grew glazed, fixed. Paige knew he couldn't see her. He wasn't seeing anything anymore.

"We have to orb him out of here," Paige said. "We have to get him to Leo. Or get Leo here!"

"By the time we get Tyler to Leo, I don't know if Leo could help him," Piper said.

"And there's still Hoptith to catch," Phoebe reminded them. "It's our fault she's on the loose. We have to make that right."

Paige could feel a sob welling up inside her chest. She knew her sisters were right. And she knew she wasn't responsible for Tyler's death. After all, he was the one who had brought them here. But in the short time she had known him, he had come to be important to her. She felt she had lost a special friend. They had shared a lot— even if she had been a cat for most of their time together.

Paige felt a cool hand on her shoulder. "His *ka* has left him," she heard.

Paige looked up into Tipket's strong face. The

woman's eyes were gentle. "Your friend is with Horus now. He was valiant, fighting on the side of good. He will be rewarded in his eternal afterlife."

"He loved it here," Paige whispered. She couldn't seem to make her voice any louder. "All he wanted was to stay."

"Would you like to see where he is now?" Tipket offered. "So you may go on your path unburdened?"

"Can you . . . can you do that?"

"Close your eyes."

Paige shut her eyes. She felt Tipket's fingers trace designs on her forehead, then on her eyes. She heard soft chanting in a language she didn't understand. Then somehow, without any sensation of moving, she was somewhere else.

She was inside an ancient tomb—one of the inner chambers of a pyramid. The walls were covered in hieroglyphics, and the room was filled with hundreds of miniature statues—of people, of animals, of objects. They were all meant as offerings for the deceased to use in the afterlife.

In front of her was an enormous lake, and she realized that it was fed by an underground river.

"Where . . . where am I?" she asked.

She heard Tipket's voice in her head, though she didn't see the high priestess in the scene before her. "The final stop on the journey to gain access to the beauties of the afterlife. This is the Hall of the Two Truths, where all the dead must face the questioner. We are in Duat, the underworld."

A door opened in the side of the chamber. Tyler stepped through it and stood, waiting. He didn't seem to notice Paige.

A terrifying creature appeared in front of her. Paige braced herself for battle. The figure had the head of a jackal but the body of a man.

"This is no demon," Tipket assured her. "This is Anubis, god of the dead."

Paige nodded, even though she didn't think Tipket was watching her. *Still, you never know.* She did notice that Tyler wasn't afraid of this strange god.

A new character materialized on a golden throne. "Osiris, lord of the underworld," Tipket's voice told her.

Paige was startled. This was the character Tyler played in the Disciples of Thoth cere-monies. They could have been twins! Osiris wore an elaborate crown, an ornate tunic and jewelry, and he carried the same kind of staff that Tyler had used in the ritual that had brought them to Egypt. Maybe Tyler was right. Maybe he was a direct descendant of this ancient society.

"Thoth, the god of wisdom, will record the result of the test."

"Test?" Paige repeated nervously. "He has to take a test?" Just the word made her anxious.

"All souls are tested before they can continue on the journey."

"Who is that?" Paige stared at an ugly beast. Its body was half lion, half hippopotamus, and it had a crocodile head. "You can't tell me that monster isn't a demon!"

"That is our most sacred Ammut."

"What does she do in the ceremony?" Paige asked, trying to stay calm.

"She will eat the hearts of those who are unworthy."

Paige gulped. *Okay, the keeping calm thing isn't really working anymore.*

"Your friend's heart will be weighed against the feather of Maat," Tipket told her. "She is the goddess of truth, divine order, and judgment."

Paige held her breath. She watched Tyler kneel before Osiris as a feather was placed on a large scale beside him. The nasty-looking creature Ammut looked way too hungry, as far as Paige was concerned.

Thoth stepped forward and wrote some notes on a papyrus roll. Osiris lifted his staff, and Tyler stood.

"That's it? Is it done?" Paige asked.

"It is done. Your friend will enjoy a happy eternity."

Tyler stepped away from the scales and walked toward the lake, where a golden boat filled with laughing and singing people glided toward him. Just before he boarded the shining ship, he turned and faced Paige. This time she knew he saw her. He smiled broadly and waved good-bye. He climbed down into the boat, where a young woman placed a floral garland on his head.

Paige felt pressure on her forehead and eyes again. The scene before her vanished. She opened her eyes, blinking a few times. "Thank you," she said to Tipket.

Piper and Phoebe embraced her. "I'm fine," she assured them, wiping a tear from her cheek. "No, I really am. He's very happy now." She took in a deep breath. "Okay. We should go look for Hoptith. Do you know where she is?"

"We think she may have gone back to our time," Phoebe said. "Maybe even our place."

"She liked Leo," Piper said. Paige could tell by her sister's tone that this didn't please her.

"She was traveling with a contemporary demon," Piper continued. "Of a type we've fought before."

"According to Cole, the pack she's hanging out with are pretty low level."

"That's good, right?" Paige asked.

"For now," Phoebe agreed. "We need to get her before she figures out who's who in the demon world and goes straight to the top."

"What should we do?" Mailin asked.

"We will stay here," Tipket declared. "She might still be in Egypt. She has scores to settle here." She taught the Halliwells the spell to bind Hoptith into her cat form and then kissed each of the girls good-bye.

Paige took her sisters' hands. "I am so ready to go home."

With Tipket adding her power to theirs, the Charmed Ones traveled back to—forward to, really—present-day San Francisco.

Paige looked around the living room. She had never been so happy to see a room in her whole life! Leo was sprawled out on the sofa, while Cole snored in the armchair.

Piper raced to Leo, and Phoebe dashed to Cole. Within moments, the men were wide awake. Dazed but awake.

"I was getting ready to orb back to get you." Leo yawned. "But I fell asleep."

Cole stretched. "I conked out too." His bleary eyes landed on Paige. "Oh. Hi, Paige. Welcome back to human."

"Thanks," Paige told him. "Are they okay?" she asked her sisters.

"It looks as if Hoptith performed only a simple sleeping spell on them," Piper surmised.

"Spell?" Leo looked puzzled.

"That was no kitty, that was a sorceress," Piper explained. She gave her husband a hug. "Lucky for you, you were just her type. It's probably why she spared you."

"She must have liked me, too," Cole pointed out. "I mean, I'm still among the living."

Phoebe kissed him and laughed. "Don't worry, honey. I think you're irresistible, even if she didn't."

"So, it's over. Everything is back to normal?" Leo asked.

"Normal for a Charmed One," Paige replied.

"Uh-oh." Cole peered at her. "What does that mean?"

"It means that we have to vanquish Hoptith by turning her back into a cat," Phoebe explained. "We unleashed her on the world. We need to get her back under control."

"Are you sure she's here?" Leo asked.

"One way to find out." Piper stood up from Leo's lap. "We can scry for her."

"Good thinking," Phoebe said. "If she's in our world, we should be able to find her. And then go after her." She found a map of the world and laid it on the coffee table. Piper opened a drawer in the cabinet and pulled out a crystal pendant. The three sisters sat on the floor. Piper held the crystal so that it dangled a few inches above the map.

"So, what was this chick like?" Paige asked. She hoped knowing a little about the enemy they were about to battle would help her when the time came.

"She's a real—," Piper began.

"Piper!" Phoebe cut her off with a warning tone.

"All I was going to say is that she's a real handful," Piper claimed innocently.

"She's powerful, she's beautiful, and she's not at all nice," Phoebe told Paige.

"Sounds like most of the demons we battle," Paige said. "Piece of cake."

"She's got a serious ego issue," Piper added. "We might be able to use that to our advantage."

"Once we find her," Phoebe said.

All three sets of the sisters' eyes were locked on the pendant. Paige's heart thudded as she watched the crystal that would tell them where the demon had gone. And then they'd have to figure out what to do with her once they found her.

"Are you looking for me?" a husky voice asked.

Paige's jaw dropped. A slim, tall beauty stood in front of them, her gold-flecked eyes flashing with indignation. *How'd that happen?* she wondered. *We were scrying, not conjuring.*

"Thanks for coming," Phoebe said. "You saved us from using up all our frequent-flier miles."

Hoptith smiled slowly. "I don't like unfinished business. And witches knowing my identity is unfinished business. So I have come here to dispose of you."

Paige stood up, ready for battle. "Uh, what is with that hair?" she said.

Piper and Phoebe stared at her.

She shrugged. "Hey, if she's so into herself, maybe it will rattle her," she whispered

"What is wrong with my hair?" Hoptith's hands fluttered to her long dark locks.

Whoa. It actually worked! "Uh . . . it's just so last year's style," Paige improvised.

"Leo thinks so too," Piper said. "Don't you, Leo?"

"The outfit, too," Leo agreed.

Hoptith spun around to glare at Leo and Piper, and Piper's hands flew up and froze her.

"Quick! The spell." Phoebe yanked Paige's hand and dragged her over to Piper. Leo and Cole stood ready, in case of any attack from those who might want to rescue Hoptith.

Which turned out to be a pretty good idea!

Chapter

17

Paige stared up toward the ceiling. The demon who had appeared was so huge, his head nearly smashed the light fixture. His bulging eyes glared down at them.

"I am here to bring back Hoptith!" he bellowed. His massive chest swelled as if he were puffing himself up.

The Halliwell sisters and their men stood gazing silently up at the demon.

Well, silence isn't going to work! Paige realized. "Keep chanting!" Paige said.

Paige's command spurred them back into action. Cole and Leo threw things at the demon, distracting him from Hoptith and the Halliwells. Paige knew the guys were trying to buy them time to finish the spell. *But what good will it do?* she worried. *The demon will just take her back to Egypt and torture Tipket until she undoes the spell!*

Or he'll grab Hoptith before we manage to bind the spell forever.

Paige recited the chant as quickly as she could, but the whole time her mind was racing, searching for alternate plans. *I should turn into a cat again,* Paige thought. *That would confuse him.*

They were nearly done with the first part of the spell—the binding part would come next. Leo and Cole had run out of ways to keep the demon occupied. The beast reached down and threw Cole across the room.

The twin cat plan would totally work, Paige was sure of it. *I should do it. I should transform myself back into a cat.*

Just as they spoke the final words of the incantation, Paige felt herself changing. The world around her got bigger as she got smaller. Her body throbbed as she went from two legs to four, and fur sprouted all over her.

I did it! Paige thought. *How is that possible? Or did I?* Could the spell they did on Hoptith have worked on her too? Since they had both been cats?

No time to think about that. The demon glared down from his enormous height. Just as Paige had hoped, seeing the two cats confused him. The size of this demon's body did not mean anything about the size of his brain.

"Where's Paige?" Piper shrieked, looking around frantically.

"If we ever needed the Power of Three to

vanquish a demon, it's now!" Phoebe said.

"Oh no!" Piper gasped, her eyes landing on Paige. "We turned her back into a cat!"

"Ah, so that is the witch. That means the other cat is Hoptith." The demon reached one of his massive hands down to grab Hoptith.

"You'll forgive me later," Paige told Piper. She hurled herself at her sister, hissing and scratching.

"Ow!" Piper flung up her hands to protect her face. "Wrong cat!"

The demon stopped for a moment, his gaze shifting from Hoptith to Paige.

I guess when they're that huge, they move more slowly, Paige observed. *Like big dinosaurs.*

She yowled at Phoebe and bit her. *Come on, Mr. Big, take the bait.*

He did. His gigantic hand wrapped around Paige's small cat body. She felt the whoosh of time travel and found herself moments later back in ancient Egypt. In fact, she realized she was back in the very same temple Tyler had brought her to.

"I will return you to your form," the demon promised. "We will have our revenge on Tipket. And then we will begin our reign"—the demon scratched her under the chin— "of chaos."

The demon strode over to the statue of Bastet, the cat-woman. "My enemy. Your days are over."

He raised his arms and began an incantation. Paige knew she had to be ready to think fast. He was about to discover his mistake, and she was pretty sure he wouldn't be happy about it.

Paige became her human self, and the demon turned to face her. The huge smile on his face faded quickly.

"Sorry, Hoptith couldn't make it," Paige declared. "My sisters still have her. I'd say she's toast by now."

"I will not be made a fool of!" the demon bellowed.

"Wanna bet?"

He charged her. *I need to tap into that shapeshifting spell,* Paige thought. *I need to transform into something as powerful as he is.* Her body rippled, and suddenly, she was a lion!

She shook her thick mane and roared. The demon skidded to a stop. Paige ran toward him, ready to tear his throat open.

She leaped on the demon and sank her teeth into his flesh. The demon howled in pain but easily knocked her off. He came at her again.

I need to get out of his reach, Paige thought. The moment she had the idea, she was a bird. She flew up and perched on the carved lotus petal at the very top of a pillar. In spite of his magnitude, the demon was far below her now.

I get the sense that the transformation back into being a cat was all my doing. And that I am capable of turning into anything. What a concept. But then it began to make sense. She had never actually tried to reverse the spell herself. She had simply assumed that she couldn't. The ritual must have been to unleash the ability of transformation, and once that happened, she could change based on her own intention.

Paige vowed to never, ever, perform a spell again without reading it through in its entirety. Only she didn't have time to mull all this over—down below her, her sisters, Leo, and Cole had just orbed in.

"We want our sister back!" Phoebe shouted up to the demon.

Piper lowered Hoptith—the cat version—to the floor. "Yeah, we're done with your pal here. You won't be unbinding this spell anytime soon."

"Paige is here," Leo said. "Somewhere."

The demon approached them slowly. He was seriously peeved. Paige swooped down from her perch, landed beside Piper, and transformed back into herself. "Hi. Anyone need a third? To round out the Power of Three?"

"I shall destroy you!" the demon bellowed. He swiped Cole up into his massive hand. Cole struggled in the creature's grip, but it was useless. It was like a toy soldier fighting with King Kong.

"The vanquishing spell, now!" Phoebe screamed.

Cole's face was getting redder and redder as the demon squeezed the life out of him. Piper tossed a glass bottle onto the floor, releasing a vanquishing potion.

We have to get through the whole incantation before we defeat this beast, Paige worried. *Cole will be dead by then!*

"Release the mortal one!" A new voice echoed throughout the temple.

Paige craned her neck and saw an astonishing sight. The cat-woman statue had come to life. And the big bad demon seemed to be afraid of her. It gave them the edge they needed.

"Creature of chaos,
We vanquish thee."

As they chanted the demon dropped Cole. He raced over to join Leo and the girls. Now that Cole was safe, Phoebe's voice grew stronger.

"Demon be gone
So that good may go free
Power of Three
Now vanquish thee.
We will forever be
Power of Three."

The demon howled, sputtered, and melted into a puddle of oozing liquid on the floor.

It was over.

The woman with the head of the cat took Paige's hand. "You were very brave. I watched all that you did. You are a worthy representative for me."

"And you are . . . ?" Paige was still confused by the whole statue coming to life thing.

"I am Bastet, the cat goddess, goddess of happy times."

"We could go for some of those happy times," Phoebe said. She slipped her arm around Cole, who kissed her.

"You will be so blessed," Bastet promised.

Tipket entered the temple. She bowed when she saw Bastet. "Honored one," she greeted.

"Faithful friend," Bastet said. "You have done my name well. I am grateful."

"We have Hoptith," Piper said. "She's all bound and everything."

"Thank you."

"No, thank you," Piper said to Tipket. "For everything you did for us."

"Those were amazing animal tricks," Phoebe said to Paige. "Brilliant idea."

"It doesn't get you off the hook for doing spells that you shouldn't," Piper scolded.

"I know. I messed up big time," Paige confessed. She decided she had to admit all. "Turning into all those animals wasn't exactly a thought-out plan," she said. "I just willed it, and it happened. Like how the orbing was before I got it under control."

"You never knew the ritual allowed you to do that, did you?" Piper said. "You didn't even read the second page."

Paige's eyebrows raised. "You knew?" she demanded. "And you didn't tell me?"

"Who had time?" Piper replied. "What with Hoptith and her demon buddies."

Phoebe stepped in between them. "I think the most important thing to remember is that Paige accomplished something major all on her own."

Paige thought about the transformations. "I used very strong intentions," she said. "I think it also helped that I had more confidence," she added.

Piper gave Paige a long look. "I suppose the only way to develop confidence is with experience."

"You mean, as in 'experimenting'?" Paige suggested.

"Carefully," Piper said. "With supervision."

"So you read the whole spell," Paige said. "Does this mean I can shape-shift anytime I want?"

"Only for as long as the original transformation ritual lasts," Piper said.

"A good thing it had staying power," Phoebe said. "Ya done good."

Paige slung her arms around her sisters' shoulders and grinned at Leo and Cole. "Can we just go home now? I have the weirdest craving for a bowl of milk."

About the Author

Carla Jablonski has edited and written dozens of best-selling books for children and young adults. She was the editor of the Hardy Boys Mystery Series and has edited two popular interactive series: Choose Your Own Adventure and RL Stine's Give Yourself Goosebumps. She is the author of several books for younger readers and for older readers she has written *Charmed: The Gypsy Enchantment* and *Clueless: Southern Fried Makeover*. Carla is also an actress, a playwright, and a trapeze artist.

SOMETHING WICCAN
THIS WAY COMES

Paige Matthews is new to the whole "Power of
Three" thing, and looking to explore her powers. So
when she reads of a Wiccan convention taking place
just outside of Las vegas, she thinks it's a great
opportunity for her *and* for her sisters to learn more
about their witchy ways. Though the girls are all
over saving innocents they aren't that heavy into
Wicca practices, and Paige thinks the retreat could
be enlightening.

Piper and Phoebe, however, aren't so sure. They're
certain that while they spend their days battling
honest-to-badness black magic, their so-called
supernatural sisters will be nothing more than
abunch of blessed wanna-bes. Soon though, they
hear of a rash of murders committed against
practicing Wiccans, and making an appearance at
the convention becomes top priority. But as they
head for the desert campgrounds, are the Charmed
Ones headed straight for disaster?